I0549054

RUNNING WITH THE BIG DOGS

Sybil Norcroft Book Six

Carl Douglass

**Neurosurgeon Turned Author
Writes with Gripping Realism**

PO Box 221974 Anchorage, Alaska 99522-1974
books@publicationconsultants.com—www.publicationconsultants.com

ISBN 978-1-59433-529-7
eISBN 978-1-59433-530-3
Library of Congress Catalog Card Number: 0000-0000

Manufactured in the United States of America.

Disclaimer

All of the six novellas in the Sybil Series are works of fiction and should not be construed as representing real persons, places, or events. Some names of real persons and places appear but only for the purpose of creating a setting in the real world or as a mention of historical circumstances. None of the real people or the real places were actually involved in the fictional portrayals found in these short books. All of the events described were created from the author's imagination.

Dedication

To my family

carldouglass.com

Books by Carl Douglass

FICTION

Last Phoenix-A Novel of Betrayal and Revenge, A Story of the CIA's Phoenix Program

Saga of a Neurosurgeon Series, **Six Books**
-Young Coyote-Book One: Garven Wilsonhulme's Way to Success-No Quarter Asked and None Given
-Anything Goes-Book Two
-Heaven and Hell-Book Three: Garven Wilsonhulme Takes on All Comers in the Jungle of Modern Competition
-Long Climb-Book Four: Young M.D., Garven Wilsonhulme, Engaged in a Social Poker Game of Winner Takes All
-Academia: The Law of the Jungle-Book Five: Surgeon in Training, Garven Wilsonhulme, Fang-and-Claw Competition for Glory
-The Vulture and the Phoenix-Book Six: Neurosurgeon, Garven Wilsonhulme, the Final Great Fight

All in Jest-Renowned Neurosurgeon in the Fight of Her Life

Gog and Magog—Yawm al-Qiyamah, Yawm al-Din, The Day of Judgment

Finders Keepers, Losers Weep-A Novel of Innocence Betrayed and the Search for Restitution

Sheep Dog and The Wolf-A Story of Terrorism and Response, and the Sheep Dogs Who Protect

Trojan Horse in the Belly of the Beast, Three Books
   Though They Come From the Ends of the Earth-Book One
   Dancing with the Devil-Book Two
   Trojan Horse in the Belly of the Beast-Book Three

NOVELLAS

1st Novella-*The End of the Beginning*

2nd Novella-*Uncharted Country, Uncertain Future*

3rd Novella-*Secrets*

4th Novella-*Secrets and Scandals*

5th Novella-*Decisions*

6th Novella-*Running with the Big Dogs*

NONFICTION

On Evolution The Origin of Selection, Order, Progression, and Diversity–out of print

Something About Religion—out of print

Chapter One

Physical Chemistry Laboratory, College Street, Main Campus, Howard University, Washington D.C., October 23, 2019

Cerisse Monet Daniels might have been an ordinary—albeit very bright—student in Chem 173 were it not for three things: She was very small, six inches smaller than the next smallest girl in the lab class. Most of the students were African-Americans, prideful of being fairly light skinned or café au lait. Cerisse was almost literally as black as coal—so black that her skin color was tending towards grey. Ordinarily at Howard University, neither her diminutive size nor her ebony color would have attracted persisting attention. However, the fact that she was accompanied by two huge guards in grey suits, white shirts, plain colored ties without designs, and scrupulously shined shoes did. All of the men on her guard detail were armed with hand guns in shoulder holsters and a second weapon in an ankle holster. They never smiled or talked to the students or the professors. Many of the Howard students considered them creepy.

Cerisse tried to fit in, to be normal; but, try as she might, she was anything but normal. Not that the other students or even her guard detail knew, but she was a pygmy born in the DRC [Democratic Republic of the Congo] and lived there until she was fourteen. During almost the entirety of her life there in the jungle, she was maltreated in the extreme. The Bantus who surrounded the pygmy villages captured her and sold her as a slave to the French. She became part of the legion of victims of human trafficking; and, among the worst of the abuses she suffered, is that she was forced into childhood prostitution. Her family and most of her relatives were massacred.

That she lived, was owing to her intrepid mother, an American doctor, who took her away and finally adopted her. Her mother and father saw her worth and potential and did all possible to get her a formal education—something she was entirely lacking in the country of her birth. Another remarkable quality of the young woman was that she was a natural linguist. From her childhood—and by necessity—Cerisse was native fluent in French (the official language of the DRC), Dutch, and Portuguese—the languages of the slave masters. She also spoke more than one dialect of Arabic and a fair share of the 242 native languages of her country, including the four national languages: Kikongo, Lingala, Swahili, and Tshiluba and some of the minor, but still important, "other languages"—Mongo, Lunda, Tetela, Chokwe, Budza, Ngbandi, Lendu, Mangbetu, Nande, Ngbaka and Eborna. Besides her exotic background, she stood out as the only African among the African-Americans. None of her classmates—all but two of whom were African-Americans—had ever actually met or mingled with a real native born African.

She came to stand out—to be different—in other ways. She was brilliant, several ticks above genius; and, despite her small and delicate appearing physique, she was a well-trained martial artist in both Brazilian Jiu-Jitsu and Krav Maga, like her mother. Sybil Norcroft—her mother, recognized that her tiny daughter would have to learn to defend herself both mentally and physically—and Cerisse excelled in both fields. Unlike her classmates, she did not strive to be popular, just to be accepted and otherwise left alone. She never flirted or played the coquette. Also, unlike her most of her classmates, she was engaged to be married to her high school sweetheart, Drake Farrer. Like Cerisse, Drake was a hard-driving, take-no-prisoners pre-med student.

Drake and Cerisse—both age nineteen—entered Howard at the same time and took almost every class together. Now, they were sophomores, and moving swiftly and successfully through the rigorous pre-medicine curriculum. Besides being engaged, in love, and immoderately helpful to one another, the two of them were in an all-out competition with each other to be Howard's valedictorian in 2021. On this particular day, they were working together to defeat everyone else in the physical chemistry laboratory course that semester.

Prior to Cerisse and Drake coming to the university, Howard produced more African—American chemists than any other chemistry department in the world. It has the largest chemistry department in the District of Columbia. It was the first predominately African-American university to grant Ph.D. degrees in chemistry. Surviving through the storms of the vicious discrimination against Negro people in the early years and the tumults of the civil rights movement, Howard was justifiably proud of its uncompromisingly rigid and rigorous standards. The professor of physical chemistry was determined that it could never be said that he was lax in his requirements of any student because of the color of their skin. He took pride in the accomplishments of his star students, and Cerisse and Drake were among them. That meant that his standards were all the more exacting upon them. The two of them thrived in that environment. They were acknowledged by their student peers to be two of the ten "A's" in the large quantitative analysis course.

The task of the day was to determine the exact amount of a compound and its nature from two unknowns the students were given. The requirement was that the weights be precise out to four decimal points. Part of doing great in the lab depended on Cerisse and Drake managing to protect their territory extremely well from the attackers who would wreck their experiments. They had gotten near-perfect scores on the mid-term written exam, one of the highest percentage scores in the professor's memory. Both of them had answered the trick questions about not analyzing heavy metal samples in an iron mortar nor storing alkali metals in glass vessels, nor exposing silver compounds to light and the technicalities of achieving a representative twenty-five gram sample of wheat from a twenty-five ton ship load. What was left to guarantee their "A's" became their main aim from then until the end of the semester. They took every security precaution to protect their lab materials from saboteurs and became justifiably paranoid in the process.

The mid-term laboratory examination was entirely open book, just a matter of determining quantities of known chemicals in a compound. Cerisse and Drake were assigned a chunk of Dolomite limestone and required to ascertain to four decimal point accuracy the quantities of the several components in the formless lump of silica, magnesium, calcium, combined oxides, and carbon dioxide. The first order of business was to determine what exactly the lump was made of. Once the relatively simple identification of the chemicals in their sample was completed, they set about to separate the parts and to weigh them with accuracy down to the ten-thousandth of a decimal point.

The test was a project expected to take a week. Cerisse and Drake had to know already to use platinum crucibles for the ignition of the contained calcium oxalate precipitates and to determine loss from ignition with professional accuracy. Porcelain crucibles were needed for the magnesium ammonium phosphate precipitates. Meker burners, blast lamps, and muffle furnaces—all of which were in short supply in the student laboratories—had to be employed; and there was going to be a lot of standing around.

It was Drake who first observed the big athletic looking light-brown guy in the vicinity of their scale. He mentioned the fellow's presence to Cerisse; so, they could be on the lookout for him if he were up to no good. Cerisse recognized him as one Howard's star football players and as one of the high scorers thus far in the class, and further, knew that the guy's scale was located all the way across the lab. He did indeed bear watching.

It was Cerisse who saw the big athlete move by the scale (number 3210) next to her's and Drake's (number 3212) and dip a moistened pair of toothpicks into the white powder sitting on the brass balance of the Mettler Scale. She did not care over much personally since it wasn't her scale but had to wonder why sabotage a lab pair who were in the middle of the pack in the class. Both she and Drake had seen similar alterations of the next-door partners' work over the last two weeks of class. Drake was for turning the guy in.

Cerisse said, "I don't like to turn anybody in to the authorities on general principles. Besides, everyone will get in a snit because my mother is famous, and I have guards. We can't let it go, but I think it's usually better to take care of your own problems. We can tell the poor schmucks at 3210, though. They can take care of it any way they like."

Drake was dubious, but agreed.

Scores were posted weekly by listing the results next to the assigned Mettler Scale numbers to preserve anonymity. For two weeks 3212 had gotten perfect scores, and Cerisse and Drake were all smiles and tranquility. 3210 got abysmal scores and those lab partners were all scowls and discomposure. The big athlete was all perplexity.

He finally could not contain himself, and heedless of the likelihood that he might be self-incriminatory, he ventured to ask Cerisse and Drake, "How'd you guys do?"

He had a peculiar Bronx accent that Cerisse thought was something that identified him as being in a mafia gang.

"Okay," replied Drake. "You get your unknowns?"

"Pretty close," the big fellow said, still uncertain of why the two lab partners were so cheerful in view of their terrible lab performance. "But I thought you hadn't done so hot."

"Actually, we were pretty lucky—got perfect scores the last two weeks," Drake added, watching the known saboteur's face.

He looked confused, unpleasantly so.

"I don't get it," he said forgetting his resolution to be subtle and not to give himself away. "I kind of thought 3210 did lousy."

"They did," Drake told him, unwilling to give out more explanatory information.

"I thought you had 3210."

"Nope."

The guy's face was earnest now. He was trying to be crafty and subtle, but it was a little late in the day for that. He did not see it though.

He kept on, "So what number are you guys?"

He was so determined in his detective work that he could not see how dumb and revealing his question was.

"Who wants to know? And how come?" asked Cerisse who had been standing to one side until now looking up at the cheating athlete's face.

Neither of the students at 3212 liked the big jerk making an obvious attempt to find out which place belonged to them; so, he could sabotage their work. The dummy might just as well have come right out and told them his plans.

The big guy knew he had kind of painted himself into a corner.

He figured—as he always did with his superior size—that a good offense was better than a good defense; so, he retorted, "Looks like you thought someone said stand-up when they said shut-up, little darkie."

Cerisse was in no mood to accept—with any measure of forgiveness—references to her size or color, certainly not in Howard University where the color of one's skin had never been allowed to influence success, and absolutely never been allowed to be used to disparage anyone. This was especially true of someone trying to wreck her and Drake's GPAs and was clumsy about it as well.

"Why don't you just go and see if you can screw up somebody else's unknown and butt out of our business, cretin?" Cerisse said.

Her secret service guards were at full attention on the small girl and the big man who appeared to be threatening her.

A small crowd was gathering, including a couple of lab instructors who had chanced to overhear the reference to sabotage. The over-muscled student was becoming uncomfortable. He did not like the reference to screwing up unknowns and the implications for his own well-being in the class; and furthermore, he did not like being called a 'cretin' even though he was not quite sure what it meant.

"How would you like to make me, little toy doll?" he sneered in a something-less-than adroit rejoinder.

Cerisse felt the eyes of the gathering crowd and especially those of Drake on her.

"This should be settled here and now. Are you threatening me?" she asked loudly enough so every student, lab tech, teacher's aide, and professor could hear.

The secret service agents moved in a little closer, not quite ready to intervene.

She was angry now. She turned to her fellow students.

"Watch this guy around your lab stuff if you want to pass this lab. Ask number 3210."

There, it was out.

The lab instructors locked eyes with the big guy, and he studied his shoes. His face was scarlet and his masseter muscles were clenched. He slowly looked over at Cerisse.

He gave her the finger and said, "You see this, pipsqueak. I can flatten you into a greasy pancake before you can say 'oh professor, dear,' and bat those scrawny little eyelashes at him."

He pantomimed a ham-sized fist on the end of an outstretched heavily muscled arm.

Cerisse's Krav Maga instructor had been in the IDF navy. In his honor she kicked her very much larger opponent square amid-ships. His eyes briefly registered consternation, then pain, and then he toppled to the floor holding on to the contents of the mid-ships stow area. Then he curled up into a fetal ball and vomited.

The larger of the two secret service guards moved extremely quickly and stood over the retching and furious man.

"Don't get up," he said quietly.

Chapter Two

White House Conference Center [an annex building of the White House], 726 Jackson Place in Washington, D.C., October 28, 2019, 0800 hrs
-Present: POTUS; VPOTUS; Surgeon General Sybil Norcroft; Attorney General; Speaker of the House; Senate Majority Leader; Secretaries of State, HHS, Treasury; Chairman CEA [Council of Economic Advisors]; Chairman, Federal Reserve Board; Chairperson, Council of Economic Advisers for the Congressional Joint Economic Committee.
Re: Impending failure to meet the year's end interest payment on the national debt.

President Parker Conrad Willets had one more year to go before his second term came to an end. Already, the 2020 election season was underway with more than the usual intensity, and there was still more than a year to go before the general election. The Democrats had seized on the latest recession as the main issue they needed to push to put them back in power in the White House, and hopefully in both houses of Congress. As usual, the causes of the recession were multi-factorial and complicated; but the collective memories of the American public were very short and poorly informed. The sitting president was at fault; one had only to become aware of two of President Willets' predecessors—George W. Bush, and Barack Obama—and their dismal popularity ratings in their second terms when they, too, were the presidents of record when a major recession gripped the country.

He greeted his serious audience in the large conference room of the annex building across the road from the White House.

"Thank you for coming. I think we have a perfect attendance today, and that bespeaks the importance of what we must discuss here. It is late in the day to mince words: we are in trouble, probably more than ever before in our history since the War of 1812. Even the grim specter of sequestration has not forced us to compromise and to cut our addiction to spending. Richard Pennyweight from Treasury, Jimmy Ropelarve from the Federal Reserve, Dwayne Fitzsimmons, from the Council of Economic Advisors, and Margaret Thampcross from the Council of Economic Advisers for the Congressional Joint Economic Committee, are here to give us the worst quarterly report in the history of the country since before the 2008 Great Recession. They will give us full reason to get our house in order. I will turn the time over to Secretary Pennyweight who will head-up the panel of expert economists. All of the fine people who will speak to us this morning are unanimous—I repeat that; unanimous—in their conclusion about what is wrong and what must be done to fix it. Secretary Pennyweight..."

Secretary Pennyweight was overweight but carried his bulk well under a perfectly custom tailored suit by Freeman

Sportsman Club in Brooklyn, his ties made by TieCrafters in Chelsea, and his shoes from John Lobbs on Madison Avenue—for the past forty years. He was quite literally a belt and suspenders man; they were made for him at Trafalgars in Manhattan. His belts were classic Newington alligators; his braces classic 100% pure woven silk. Pennyweight's most important nod to vanity and his least obvious were his human hair wigs from Lugos on Dyckman Street. He hated the male pattern baldness that left him with a monk's tonsure look that aged him ten years. He was 62 but looked 48 after his face lift and with his perfectly coifed light-brown toupee.

"My fellow Americans," he began, "I address you this way because we have an American problem—not a Republican or Democrat, or urban or rural, or rich or poor, problem. The directors of the federal government councils of economic advisors, the best minds at treasury and the Fed, and a host of objective university economists, are for the first time in my memory, unanimous in our findings and opinions. Our economy—as we now know it—will not serve us five years from now if we do not get it under control. In fact, if we default on our loans from the Chinese, that change will be upon us for all practical matters in January of 2021. We will take the blame for the consequences, whether we are truly responsible or not. Capitalism and market economic practices have failed us. Greed has not been good. Keynesian economics has failed us; our episodic coziness with socialistic economic experiments has failed us. We have learned beyond doubt that we cannot spend our way into prosperity.

"After prolonged studies of the American democracy, either Alexis de Tocqueville in 1835 or Alexander Fraser Tytler, Lord Woodhouselee, in 1790, expressed their evidence-based criticism of the economic stability of democracies. In essence, what they said was, 'a democracy is always temporary in nature; it simply cannot exist as a permanent form of government. A democracy will continue to exist up until the time that voters discover that they can vote themselves generous gifts from the public treasury. From that moment on, the majority always votes for the candidates who promise the most benefits from the public treasury, with the result that every democracy will finally collapse due to loose fiscal policy. They went on to point out that the average age of the world's greatest civilizations from the beginning of history has been about 200 years... always to be followed by a dictatorship.'

P. J. O'Rourke put it more succinctly and pithily, 'A government with the policy to rob Peter to pay Paul can be assured of the support of Paul, and giving money and power to government is like giving whiskey and car keys to teenage boys.' The PRC [Peoples Republic of China]—which owns more than 60% of our debt—stands fully ready to solve our problem for us.

"One does not have to be an historian to see the truth which de Tocquefulle and Tytler said. You hardly have to look back ten years. Our government bodies cannot agree on policies critical to the survival of our nation. Republicans spend us into penury on military gadgetry and support of fat cats. Democrats have created entitlements for their constituents who are the poor, the needy, the handicapped, the unionists, the pensioners, the illegal immigrants, and on and on. Until the past year, each succeeding presidential administration and change in Congress has solved the problem in two ways: kick the stone on down the road for a few years and borrow. We have not been able to pay anything on the principle of our indebtedness for two decades. And now, my fellow Americans, we may not be able to pay even the quarterly interest we owe.

"Mark my words, we will make drastic changes in the next two months, or the tide of history will wash over us, and the America we know will be irretrievably altered. We are not going to like any solution we come up with here, but we will hate the results of failure to act responsibly. I will open the session to the other experts now with the question: irrespective of political reverberations, what can we do? Or more to the point, what must we do?"

The Chairman CEA [Council of Economic Advisors], William Sizemore, spoke next in answer to Secretary Pennyweight's query: "I'll quote Tytler again. He wrote a profound treatise on the causes of the downfall of the Athenian democracy. He said, 'Nor were the superior classes in the actual enjoyment of a rational liberty and independence. They were perpetually divided into factions, which servilely ranked themselves under the banners of the contending demagogues; and these maintained their influence over their partisans by the most shameful corruption and bribery, of which the means were supplied alone by the plunder of the public money.' That's us in a nutshell. So, the first thing we must do as officials united in the effort to stave off this impending disaster, is to effect a radical change in how our government functions—down with greed and the incessant electioneering, and up with the sweaty and unpopular work of cutting pork and adding to the austerity program with an increase in taxes—not just the 'tax the rich' concept that has become the Republican mantra, but raise taxes across the board. Everyone is going to have to hurt."

The Speaker of the House, Sanjay Sengupta took his turn, "I want to be re-elected as much as the next person, but we can no longer keep on having one or the other party constantly attacking the other at the expense of the American people. I have reluctantly come to the personal conclusion that I am not significant enough that I must be re-elected to my current post or to be elected president, and it is high time that the rest of the elected officials agree with that sentiment. Tomorrow, we need to get term limits, ethics, and seniority preferences limitations, legislation under way. We have to stop our eleventh hour brinkmanship, earmarks, and other non-budgetary gimmicks. Regrettably, the by-product of this budget gamesmanship is a dramatic reduction in genuine tax policy consideration; and we can no longer afford to do that.

"We on the Democrat side of the aisle of the House are as concerned as the loyal opposition on the right. Acting in my role as Speaker of the House, I will introduce an omnibus bill that will make earmarks illegal, among other things. Earmarks reflect a broken budget process and reward frank dishonesty. Almost always earmarks reward parochial interests at the expense of national needs. The earmarking process also often subverts established merit-based, competitive, or formula-driven budget processes without debate. Ultimately earmarks may fund projects many people consider worthy enterprises for the public to pursue, but the earmark process does not guarantee these are the *most* beneficial and worthwhile projects for the nation or the project that warrants priority. I have a bipartisan group of blue dog Democrats who are forming a caucus with moderately centric Republicans to get ethics legislation before the Congress which will include serious efforts to adopt term limits. These changes are so sweeping that we will probably have to get a constitutional amendment through—maybe more than one."

Vice-President Tanner L. Oldroyd spoke next, "Secretary of State Thompson Kennedy and I have had a secret meeting with PRC Chairman Liew Bao-Zhi in Beijing two weeks ago. He and the Politburo Standing Committee of the Communist Party of China have agreed in principle to give us an extension of the deadline for payment of the interest owed them for one year on condition…"

"What conditions?!" demanded Margaret Thampcross, the most fiscally liberal of all the members of the Congressional and Executive economic advisors.

"Unpalatable ones, I regret to say; but nothing more than we should be ready to do ourselves. They are brief: First, the next budget of the United States will have a no-new-debts provision; and we must enact legislation that guarantees a balanced budget in two years. Second, beginning with the budget of 2022, a provision must be placed in every succeeding budget that a 10% payment of our national debt principal is included until the entire debt is cleared. Third, we will cease any governmental rhetoric critical of the PRC."

Secretary Kennedy said, "I know it seems almost impossible to meet the demand that we no longer exercise our constitutional right to freedom of speech when it comes to the Chinese, but that requirement was a good deal less onerous that the alternative they initially presented. Chairman Liew told us right up front that if we failed in any part of those three requirements that the PRC would call due the principle of our debt—all of it. That debt now totals just over $18 trillion of which 60 plus percent is owed the Chinese. $18 trillion is equal to the GDP of the communist Chinese nation. Richard Pennyweight from Treasury, Jimmy Ropelarve from the Federal Reserve, Dwayne Fitzsimmons, from the Council of Economic Advisors, and Margaret Thampcross from the

Council of Economic Advisers for the Congressional Joint Economic Committee or just about any university professor of economics or most well-informed persons on the street can tell you without hesitating that we don't have anything like that kind of money."

"And, we will be bankrupt the next day," Ropelarve said in his usual dour manner.

"There will be a firestorm in the country, widespread unemployment, failed businesses, and bread lines," Margaret Thampcross added morosely, "but as bad as that will undoubtedly be, nothing compares to the specter of U.S. bankruptcy and the greatest and longest depression that the world will ever see, if we don't do what we know we must and do it starting tomorrow."

Sybil Norcroft, M.D., Ph.D., F.A.C.S., the Surgeon General, added another grim reality, "The days of business-as-usual in medical care delivery are over. The best and the brightest people in academic medicine and in the world of major health care delivery have come up with lists of what they call 'impossible problems' for which they believe there are solutions that would take time, but which they believe will work. Consider just a few: for all its good intentions, the PPACA [Patient Portability and Affordable Care Act] or 'Obamacare' as it is known pejoratively, has failed. I could talk all day about why. Equally, and lamentably, capitalism or 'the market-place'—as the Tea-Partiers like to term it—has also failed and that failure worsens daily. We do not deliver the best medical care in the world or even good care for our lower socioeconomic strata. This year alone, one-third of all of the patients in our so-called healthcare system—which incidentally does not provide care to 45 million people at all and is not a system by any definition in the world—harmed one-third of the patients who came asking for care. We spend nearly $30 trillion a year, and even conservative estimates indicate that more than $800 billion were wasted. Mind you, ladies and gentlemen, that figure starts with a 'B'. It is obvious that just eliminating duplication, waste, and fraud, would go a significant ways to pay off our onerous debt. I have a proposal that is as terrible as any yet tendered here today and as necessary."

President Willets looked at Sybil earnestly.

"Dr. Norcroft, we need to hear your proposal, but the hour is getting late. Let us all think on this and meet again tomorrow morning. Can you have the necessary information ready for us by then?"

"HHS Secretary Margoles and I have already prepared a white paper with all of the data to support our proposal. We can give a presentation tomorrow; but, be warned, Mr. President, it will take a couple of hours; and it will be technical. It should also be extremely persuasive."

"I would expect nothing less from you, Dr. Norcroft. I'll try and get a good rest tonight to be able to listen to numbers."

Chapter Three

House No. 6, Maly Patriarshy Pereulok, South-west Side of Patriarshiye Ponds, Moscow, Home of Leonid Aleksandrovich Zaslavsky, the *vory v zakone* [syndicate boss and chief of the thieves-in-law] of the *Solntsevskaya Bratva, russkaya mafiya* [Russian mafia], October 28, 2019, 1100 hrs

Renata Leonidovna Zaslavsky—the only daughter of the chief of the "thieves-in-law" as the Russian mafia termed their family driven crime syndicate—entered the family room and sat on the arm of Leonid's favorite overstuffed chair and positioned her long legs on the ottoman.

"Daddy," she said, "I have an idea…"

"Oh, no, Renatya," the huge bear of a man said, pressing is head against her shoulder as if to hide his eyes in fear, "I know this is going to cost me dearly."

She knew she had him when he used the family's affectionate diminutive for her.

"The boys and I having been doing a little mining."

"Um hummh," Leonid said, his interest now piqued, "and what did you dig up?"

"We hacked into the U.S. Treasury internal site and found a series of encrypted e-mails between Treasury and the Fed. Once Afanasy and Lyosha were able to decyrypt the information, we got reams of paper on the failing financial institutions in America. The long and the short of it is that they might not be able to make their next interest payments on their national debt, and there will be a catastrophic drop in U.S. stocks, bonds, and the money market. There were suggestions of austerity programs, but neither Pennyweight nor Roperlarve was specific about what they might recommend to Willets. The date is clear however: the interest payment comes due on January first next year."

"And—like always—they will find a way to kick the can down the road," the elder Zaslavsky said giving a nod to the history of U.S. economic policy.

"Even presuming that, Daddy, they cannot continue that deficit spending forever. Right now, they owe the Chinese something like $108 billion, and the number increases exponentially every year. If they default, they will never get back to their original powerful economy, and all of the rest of the world will suffer as well."

"Even us. That can't be a good thing for business, my brainiac daughter."

"Oh, but with all respect, honored father..."

Leonid rolled his eyes.

"What I was going to say, Sir, is that while all of the unsuspecting world suffers, we can profit beyond our wildest imaginations."

"I suppose you and the boys know just how to do that."

"We do," she said smugly.

President Afonasii Glebovich Tikhondnko's Office, Royal Apartments in the Terem Palace, The Kremlin, Moscow, *Rossiyskaya Federatsiya*, October 28, 2019, 1630 hrs Present: President Tikhondnko; Boris Petrovich Orloff, Prime Minister of Russia; Andrei Levinovich Yudin, Chairman of the Federation Council of Russia [Upper house of the Federal Assembly of Russia]; Vadim Turchinevich Simonich, Chairman of State Duma Council [lower house of the Federal Assembly of Russia]; Rodian Stankevich, Minister of Finance; Colonel General Yevgeni Mitrokhin, Director of the SVR [Foreign Intelligence Service]; Michael Levinovich Ledvinov, Director of the MVD [Ministry of Internal Affairs];

Having had three attempts on his life in as many years, President Tikhondnko had devised a number of curious security measures. In order to ensure that no one carrying a weapon came to a state meeting with him, he introduced the pleasant custom of having all men share a *banya* [traditional Russian steam bath] with him and all women share a *banya* with his wife, Eugenia. For the important men who answered the president's summons that brisk fall day, it was something of a leveling experience, and a daunting reminder that even they might be suspect. It therefore became a comfort to enter the *banya*; there was a very low potential that a violent act with a weapon would result.

In his office, President Tikhondnko had his steward serve two fingers of expensive Alizé vodka neat to each of the attendees, then started the meeting without further informalities, "Director Ledvinov had a very interesting call from house No. 6, Maly Patriarshy Pereulok, this afternoon. We have had a chance to verify the information. I'll let Michael Levinovich give you the whole story."

The Director of the MVD was a wizened old man of small stature who commanded respect from everyone in the government, fear in most them, and in all of the public. When he talked—which was seldom—people who mattered, listened. This was one of those times.

"Gentlemen, comrades, I received a call from House No. 6, Maly Patriarshy Pereulok, at 1421 hours today. Leonid Aleksandrovich offered the government a very interesting proposition. He told me that some of his compatriots have discovered secure financial information from American sources that indicate an impending melt-down of their economy. As near as they can tell at this point, the fall from power is inevitable."

"Let me guess," Colonel General Mitrokhin said, "those 'compatriots' would be none other than his beautiful and brilliant daughter, Renata Leonidovna, Afanasy Fedoseev, and Lyosha Demidov."

"The same," Ledvinov said, "while we were discriminating against them flagrantly, Zaslavsky and his Mafiosi studied them and selected out the bright ones. They were children of the streets abandoned by their prostitute mothers when they became inconvenient. They were discovered by the *russkaya mafiya* when they were still prepubescent. Recognizing talent—even genius—when they saw it, the Mafiosi had the boys educated in everything that had to do with computers. They gave them last names; as you recall, Russian people began receiving surnames only about 100 years ago during the first population census of 1897. Until that time, all that passed for a last name was a nickname, and many of those in villages were absurd and even demeaning. Both boys—Afanasy and Lyosha—were arbitrarily given surnames of senior Mafiosi. Neither boy had a patronymic because neither had a father.

"The boys were given status and treated well but were more or less prisoners in gilded cages in their early years as junior Mafiosoi. As time went on, and they grew older; they also grew craftier; and finally, they became minor *russkaya mafiya* princes and were allowed considerable latitude for travel and social activities. They have had three hard and fast rules of life: no drugs or alcohol in a land and industry rife with addiction, no freedom from their watchers/body guards ever, and no betrayal of the *russkaya mafia*—early on they learned that use of their talents against their benefactors was considered to be a capital crime. Like other young hackers, they enjoyed their lives as princes and had no thought of killing the goose that was laying their golden eggs. The two boys have reveled in their status as top hackers in the computer underground community.

"Any expense put out for them has returned the Zaslavsky family a thousand-fold of profit. The present proposition sounds like more of the same. I want you to realize that what I am about to tell you is lacking in details. Those details are what the Americans call 'trade or proprietary secrets', and they belong to the Zaslavskies. They are willing to share, but they continue to hold the linch-pin elements.

"They have people in strategic places in the stock markets—New York, San Francisco, Los Angeles, Boston, Chicago, you name it. All the hackers have to do is to send a sell order and a poorly performing stock will slide towards oblivion only to be purchased on what is known as a 'short sale' or 'shorting'. It is complicated, but in essence short selling is going against the upward trend of the stock market. The practice is most commonly done with financial instruments traded in public securities, futures, or currency markets, due to their liquidity. Speculators sell short in the hope of realizing a profit on an instrument which appears to be overvalued, and that is where our insider information comes in. We know that almost all stocks are going to go into free fall, which ones will go down first, and which ones will yield the most profit. As decadent America gets its comeuppance, our Russian financial institutions, the government, and, of course, the Mafiosi, will reap the obscene profits. In a sudden leap—which will take place in less than a year—we will replace the United States at the top of the heap and will trump out the Chinese who have been expecting to take that place gradually as the U.S. takes the plunge. The morons in the PRC just don't have the educational background to operate at this level."

"I hate to appear to be one of those 'morons', Comrade Michael Levinovich; but I need a little clarification of how this grand scheme works," said Boris Petrovich Orloff, Prime Minister of Russia.

"Happy to oblige, Comrade Boris Petrovich. The process is rather complicated; and, on the surface, seems counter-intuitive. One sells financial instruments such as securities that one does not as yet own. Then, later, one repurchases them. The bet is that the price will decline during that period between selling and rebuying. If that proves to be correct, the person 'selling short' profits and pays off the original costs. Of course, should the financial instrument rise in value, the short seller loses; and the loss could be unlimited if the instrument rises in value with no end in sight. In practice, the individual selling short is required to post collateral to cover potential losses. If the individual fails to do so, then the broker liquidates the short seller's position; and the losses are covered. Usually the seller must borrow the securities in order to manipulate the delivery of the short sale. Sometimes, in the U.S. the seller must pay a fee to borrow, and must reimburse the lender for any losses.

"Historically, the returns over many decades have been approximately 10% profit; but, in the case of well understood short selling—such as having insider information—the profits can be colossal. Short selling—especially in times of economic recessions—is very much frowned upon, but not illegal. In short, because we know that the stock and securities markets are going to plummet in the next several months, we can expect to profit at rates exceeding 100%. Frankly, Comrade Boris Petrovich, we in the government do not have the technical expertise to succeed as short sellers; but our 'friends'—the Zavlavskies—do; and we need them. Joining forces with them on a short-term basis will be what the Americans refer to as a win-win proposition."

The prime minister said, "So, our risks are that this is illegal; and we could be exposed; we could be wrong about what the Americans are doing; and the markets could remain stable and not fail; and we would lose our figurative shirts and be exposed as financial terrorists."

"Not really, Sir. The Zaslavskies and their lackeys will be the only public face. Even in the event of the failures you suggest, all we will lose is money; and our part will remain hidden."

President Tikhondnko looked around the room with a questioning face. The faces looking back at him were all registering an affirmative expression.

"Then, let us get into bed with the devil," the president ordered.

Chapter Four

White House Conference Center [an annex building of the White House], 726 Jackson Place in Washington, D.C., October 29, 2019, 0800 hrs
-Present: POTUS; VPOTUS; Surgeon General Sybil Norcroft; Attorney General; Speaker of the House; Senate Majority Leader; Secretaries of State, HHS, Treasury; Chairman CEA [Council of Economic Advisors]; Chairman, Federal Reserve Board; Chairperson, Council of Economic Advisers for the Congressional Joint Economic Committee.
Re: Proposal to create a National Health Service to forestall impending failure of the United States economy.

President Willets opened the meeting on an upbeat note, "I have been in contact with PRC Chairman Liew Bao-Zhi by telephone last evening and again this morning. It is in their best interests to support us on a temporary basis. He insists on absolute secrecy about the PRC's involvement. His conservative wing would have his head if they knew that he was going to allow an opportunity to destroy the power of the United States pass without jumping on it. They know next to nothing about geopolitical finances, and would never be able to grasp the fact that destroying the U.S. economy would plunge their own rapidly developing nation into the doldrums for decades to come as well. Now, it is time for us to hear from Frank Margoles from HHS and Dr. Norcroft, the Surgeon General."

Dr. Margoles smiled and indicated that Dr. Norcroft would make the presentation since it was more or less her baby.

"Thank you, Dr. Margoles, Mr. President, and all of you. I have been working on this for several years. Allow me a moment to let you know how I got interested. I have five friends—middle-aged independent practitioners of cardiology—whose business operates in the red despite them having a thriving clinical practice. I, like you, had to ask, how can that be? The answer is simple, and chilling. Nonhospital clinicians in subspecialties such as cardiology, neurosurgery, orthopedics, urology, etc. cannot collect enough on their billing to make ends meet. They are leaving private practice in droves. However, hospitals and other large health organizations can only hire so many physicians; and, because supply of physicians applying for those jobs outstrips the demand offered by the HMOs and hospitals is now quite low, the only alternative for my friends and doctors like them is to retire early and usually to get new jobs outside of medicine. That flies in the face of a critical shortage of doctors to serve our population and constitutes healthcare delivery nonsense.

Newly graduated physicians are in an even worse position. They have mountains of debt, and decent jobs are not available. Many of them will never practice clinical medicine and even insurance companies and large corporations are overstaffed by overqualified medical personnel. The patients out there in the country are having real difficulty obtaining a doctor. Physicians' assistants and nurse practitioners cannot absorb the whole load because—although they are fine people—their educations are limited; and crucial skills possessed by physicians are becoming less and less available.

"The PPACA [Patient Portability and Affordable Care Act of 2010, or "Obamacare", as it is pejoratively known] has failed miserably to deliver on its promise. The concepts were excellent: patient centered health care delivery systems managed by a number of different accountable care organizations; payment based not on fee-for-service, but rather on evidence based performance and efficiency; bringing into the system the forty million uninsured who were—and, unfortunately, still are—clogging our emergency rooms.

This included a mandatory agreement by all Americans to have insurance and therefore to remove 'free-riders' from the equation which would go a long ways to alleviate costs of our system. Better preventative care and better early care would prevent paying the huge costs of taking care of late stage problems, especially in chronic diseases. Better life-style decisions on the part of better educated patients would help to eradicate the health consequences of obesity, high blood pressure, diabetes, sedentary life styles and the like.

More family practitioners and nurse practitioners and physicians would be available to take care of patients earlier and better to lessen the impetus to be treated by expensive specialists. Doctors, hospitals, insurance companies, drug and medical device companies would unite in their own best interests to improve the health of the nation and to reduce our skyrocketing costs. Waste, fraud, over usage, defensive medicine, and a host of other evils would be eliminated.

"However, the PPACA had three fatal flaws that doomed it from the beginning; and the rate of decline of our health care system has not improved, nor has its role as a driving force towards national bankruptcy been removed. At the get-go, the Affordable Care Act was guaranteed to fail because it was conceived in partisan politics and its qualities were determined by a win and lose Democrat versus Republican stand-off. Second, no viable provision was made to deal with medical malpractice; the American Trial Lawyers Association won that issue—a Democrat victory which resulted in the continuation of defensive medicine, waste, corruption, and over usage for self-protection of the doctors, nurses, and hospitals. The final major flaw, and one rife with secrets, lies, and corruption, was that the insurance companies were allowed—or, more accurately, they prevailed, because of their enormous financial power—to continue business as usual. The president promised, lied, and obfuscated. The insurance companies quietly dropped patients who were sick or old or poor—so much for the portability portion of the PPACA. The most egregious action by the insurance companies was to raise premiums as much as triple, and to decrease coverage by foisting incredibly high deductibles on the unsuspecting and struggling middle class. The most telling symptoms of the sickness of the PPACA is that unfortunate middle class citizens are electing to pay an unproductive fine or as the Supreme Court termed it, "a tax," rather than go broke trying to pay for their family's insurance premiums.

"The Republicans won that part of the political struggle; and between them, the two parties made great strides towards wrecking the middle class thereby reducing the nation's tax revenues and its ability to pay on the principle of the national debt or even the interest. Ladies and gentlemen, we have been going around trying to milk a duck for years. It is time to quit, to remove decent medical care from the greed and politics of the capitalist market place, and to provide a simple, honest, efficient, evidence based, single payer, health insurance system. We have never had a 'system'. It is time, posthumous, that we did; and its form needs to be a National Health Care System. We need to stop the national angst over having a 'socialized' medicine system like the rest of the civilized world."

In the next three weeks—and with the close observation of the Chinese—the legislative, judicial, and executive branches of the United States federal government pushed through measures that: raised taxes 10% across the board, established a National Health Service with the help of Canada, cut federal spending by 30% in every department and bureau. In addition a new security force was established which was tasked with ferreting out waste and fraud in every government agency and project with enough of a law-enforcement presence to investigate and to prosecute tax cheats, Medicare and Medicaid frauds, and price gouging by all vendors serving the system.

It was not a smooth beginning; but it was a beginning; and in short order individual state governments joined the struggle. The gears of government grind slowly; but, after the president declared a national emergency and caused a low-grade panic among the citizenry, it was amazing how rapidly change could be brought to pass by an aroused public. Americans are slow to anger, and reluctant to make large changes; but, in contrast to their usual apathy and contrariness, the members of the American democracy are very good at reacting positively to a real crisis.

One aspect of the lack of smoothness was the irate response by some citizens and their political representatives as diverse as the hard-core unionists and pension fund managers in the East and the Tea-Party die-hards in the Southeast and West of the Great Plains. The president and vice-president, Sybil Norcroft, Frank Margoles, Speaker Sengupta, and Senate Majority Leader Randolph Coombs bore the brunt of a firestorm of criticism. However, this time—unlike the previous most unpopular measures championed by many of the same national leaders to gain control of the H_5N_1 influenza pandemic—the federal and state officials did not disagree in private with the measures to save the country; so, no impeachment movement gained momentum. However, there were very serious threats made against any and everyone who was responsible for the extremely unpopular austerity measures. Sybil Norcroft, former neurosurgeon, and Georgetown wife and mother was shortly to learn the degree to which those threats would be carried.

SEC Enforcement Division Office, SEC Headquarters, 100 F Street, NE, Washington, D.C., November 12, 2019, 1000 hrs

The daily reports from the floor of the New York Stock Exchange bored most of the SEC agents because they were monotonous—day after day, the same bland reports of routine buying and selling. John Bridger Warden was different. He had the eye of a gem cutter and the soul of an accountant. He loved looking at the reports, and his greatest excitement in a given day was to find the discrepancy—the crime.

November 12 started off as more than routine. Several Floor officials at the NYSE had sent reports of suspicious activity to the MSD [Market Surveillance Division] of the exchange—

the regulation division responsible for monitoring trading activities on the floor and the records of trading by member firms of NYSE-listed securities. The MSD flagged a series of what appeared likely to be trading abuses and recommended formal investigation by the NYSE Regulation's Enforcement Division. Randy St. James in enforcement flagged over 100 highly suspicious short sales and sent his report on to the officer of the day, John Bridger Warden, with a note telling Agent Warden that NYSE was opening a formal investigation; and the SEC would likely want to be involved. He forwarded a copy of the report and the Regulation's Enforcement Division's preliminary findings and conclusions to the FBI.

Warden poured over the raw data and referred frequently to the new SEC OCIE [Office of Compliance Inspections and Examinations] Risk Alerts to detect and thereby to prevent options trading that circumvents SEC short-sale rules. He found 128 instances of options trading that seemed to have been executed for that very purpose. The regulation dubbed "SHO" tightened requirements for short sales of borrowed securities. Warden knew that short sales are legal and that short sellers are allowed to profit from price declines by replacing borrowed securities at a lower price.

SHO required short sellers who fail to deliver securities after the settlement date to close out their position immediately, unless they qualify as bona fide market makers for a limited amount of extra time to close-out; and none of that day's short sellers appeared to fall into that category. Agent Warden checked each trade against the regs to see if the trading strategies observed by the OCIE staff only gave the *impression* of satisfying the SHO "close-out requirement," while in effect evading it. These 128 trades appeared to be sham close-outs that violate the SEC rule, which was written to ensure that trades settle promptly, thereby reducing settlement failures.

Agent Warden alerted his counterparts at the FBI, MSD, and Andrew Grantland from the New York Regional Office by a Go-to-Meeting electronic conference after a two hour scrutiny of the trades. The trading day had hardly even begun.

"Amil, you on the line?"

"I am, John," answered Amil Sondregger, the SAC of the FBI's east coast securities fraud division.

"Erick, are you with us?"

"I can hear everyone perfectly. The Go-to-Meeting set up is working perfectly. I am reading your highlighted trades as we are talking," Erick Nielsen, chief at MSD, said.

"I'm with you guys. This Go-to-Meeting hook-up is working perfectly. I have eight officers here at Brookfield Place on Vesey Street huddled around the screen. We're all ready," Andrew Grantland said.

"All right, then, you guys," Agent Warden said, "this is what I'm seeing. We have 128 instances of fairly flagrant failures of the 'close-out requirement' by evasive options trading. There are more short sales violations coming in even as we are talking on the phone. I am watching my computer screen, and picking out one or two a minute. I am probably missing two or three times that many.

"The most worrisome ones are truly abusive naked short sales—out-and-out securities fraud in which stocks are being sold without ever being borrowed and without any apparent effort to borrow. We are seeing a blitz of 'short-and-distort' false information to drive down stock prices artificially. Losses by companies like AT&T, GM, Chrysler, Delta Airlines, AIG, and Walmart—to name a few—are soaring as a result of a very cleverly arranged misinformation program. The misinformation looks superficially like intra-company communications that hint at a severe bear market for their stocks because of expected failing year-end mandatory reports. If it were true, we would be looking at widespread insider trading. If the advertising whisper campaign is false—as we are all but certain is the case—it is felonious activity designed not only to injure a company and thereby to profit, but the intent appears to be to wreak real havoc on the securities markets as a whole."

"How many different traders, and what companies do they represent?" Nielsen asked.

"Is this coordinated?" Grantland asked.

"It's too early to be certain," Warden answered, "but it smells of fish. That's my gut feeling but a lot more than a hunch at this point...Hang on, a moment, I've got an updated list coming in from my agents..."

There was a three minute pause.

"Sorry about that. I have bad news and worse news. The numbers of counts are escalating beyond anything any of us could imagine. We now have a list of crimes as long as your arm: there are fifty new counts of trading exclusively in hard-to-borrow securities and threshold list securities; twenty-two for trading in near-term listed options on that kind of securities; a dozen and a half large short positions in hard-to-borrow securities or threshold list securities; eighty-six more large failures to deliver positions in accounts, most of them in multiple securities; 188 counts of continuous failure to deliver positions; two score counts of using buy-writes, married puts, deep in-the-money buy-writes or married puts, to satisfy the close-out requirement.

"Most of those buy-writes have little to no open interest aside from that trader's activity, resulting in all or nearly all of the call options being assigned. There have been at least fifty cases of theft from investors by outright embezzlement by stockbrokers and stock manipulation. Our internet monitors have alerted us to more than 300 internet "pump and dump" schemes.

"We have twenty-six confirmed counts of trading in customizable FLEX options in hard-to-borrow securities and/or threshold list securities. Many of those are very short-term FLEX options. We have identified a bunch of probable market makers trading in hard-to-borrow or threshold list securities claiming the option exception from the locate requirement of SHO; these traders haven't made markets in these securities. They just make trades only to take advantage of the option mispricing. We have seven known traders who have succeeded in making multiple large trades with the same trader acting as a contra party in *several* hard-to-borrow or threshold list securities. It appears that several of these traders are assisting each other to avoid having to deliver shares. These actions cannot possibility be coincidental. We don't have this many fraudulent trades in two years, let alone in two days."

"How much money are we talking about, Agent Warden?" Andrew Grantland asked.

"Well, sir, in an average year we see something on the order of $10 to maybe $20 billion in fraudulent trades. The most I have ever seen in a single year was about $40 billion, to the best of my recollection. This is still an accounting nightmare, but even a conservative estimate of the level of theft in the last two days is in excess of $200 billion. I stress the use of the adjective, 'conservative'."

"Do you have any clear-cut evidence of collusion?" SAC Sondregger asked very seriously.

That would mandate involvement by the Federal Bureau of Investigation.

"Not for sure. I have only had an hour and a half to gather information, but there are some suggestive findings. First, many of the traders have eastern European surnames—the majority of which are Slavic or Russian. Second, they all seem to be independent day traders with no business connection with one another. That is a coincidence of the highest order, and I am pretty much allergic to the very concept of coincidence. Third, many of the names of the traders are phonies—which is a red-flag raiser, if ever there was one. Fourth—and this is just my preliminary take—someone is pulling the strings, and that someone has to be extremely well-connected with a motley assortment of shady traders."

"Organized crime?"

"The Chinese?"

"Let me try out an answer to that," said Andrew Grantland from the New York Regional Office. "U.S. criminal syndicates have considerable sophistication, but hardly the know-how to organize such a complicated effort. Besides, it is counter-intuitive for them. They need the NYSE and regional stock exchanges to launder their ill-gotten gains and to turn their profits in crime to legitimate earnings which are above suspicion.

The Chinese have a very sophisticated cyber hacking and cybertage capability and could feasibly pull this off. The government and the Fed are convinced that the PRC is desperate to ensure the U.S. economy—especially the stock markets—to preserve their investments. An injury to the U.S. economy of this order of magnitude would be a catastrophe for them. They would be shooting themselves in the foot if they did anything like this. It is easier to imagine a disgruntled U.S.

federal agent or an angry Tea-Partier or union boss who thinks the present administration is going to destroy his union's entitlements, or an exasperated Milton Friedman-type intent on making a point about how inefficient democracy is doing such a suicidal thing.

"Obviously, I don't think any of those scenarios is reasonable. But consider the possibility that someone in the *russkaya mafiya* has a more-or-less pure motive to steal on the grandest scale ever accomplished in the history of the world and is completely lacking in conscience."

"Now, that's believable," muttered MSD Chief Erick Nielsen.

"I think there is a flaw in the reasoning," said SAC Sondregger, "while I know that the Russian Mafia is heartless and totally ruthless in its practices, they still have to operate with some level of approval by the Russian Federation. It seems unlikely to me that the Russian government would give even a 'wink-wink, nod-nod' to such a monstrous plan. None of this makes complete sense. I admit, however, that there has to be a major player whose identity is illusive for now."

Agent Warden countered, "With all due respect, Special Agent Sondregger, over here on F Street, we think that the Russians *are* aware of something of which we have only had glimpses. They have hacked our military, federal government, and financial industry computer systems for years. That is a given and is the equivalent of the planting of listening device in the walls of the U.S. Embassy in Moscow—which came to be known as the 'bug house' in later years—by the Soviets insisting that only good Russians be hired to design and construct the embassy in 1988. If they know—that is, if they have the deepest of insider information—from the U.S. government that a near financial collapse is in the offing—they may be willing to embark on an extreme tactic of adventurism. In fact, they may be willing to partner up with one of the most powerful and effective of the *russkaya mafiya* outfits."

"Like the *Solntsevskaya Bratva,*" SAC Sondregger said, beginning to accept the hypothesis that Agent Warden was weaving. "Our cyber watch people have identified Leonid Aleksandrovich Zaslavsky as the *vory v zakone* [syndicate boss and chief of the thieves-in-law] of Russia's largest criminal group. They have somewhere north of 5,000 members, and they have a global reach. Interpol described the Solntsevo district *mafiya* as one of the best structured criminal organizations in Europe and that it operates as a quasi-military operation. The FBI indicated that Russian-speaking criminal syndicates control a third of the estimated $12 billion global cybercrime market. They have the best hackers in the world on their payroll. They would seem to be fully capable of pulling this off. All they would need to proceed is the tacit approval of President Afonasii Glebovich Tikhondnko."

"It boggles the mind," Andrew Grantland said, speaking for all of them. "We need to get this to the DFBI, the DOJ [Department of Justice], and the president."

Chapter Five

White House Conference Center [an annex building of the White House], 726 Jackson Place in Washington, D.C., November 13, 2019, 0800 hrs
PDB [President's Daily Briefing]
-Present: POTUS; VPOTUS; Attorney General; Speaker of the House; Senate Majority Leader; Secretaries of State and Treasury; DFBI; DCIA; Chairman CEA [Council of Economic Advisors]; Chairman, Federal Reserve Board; Chairperson, Council of Economic Advisers for the Congressional Joint Economic Committee; Director Homeland Security Computer Emergency Response Team—Industrial Control Systems Cyber Emergency Response Team [ICS-CERT]; Director National Cyber Investigative Joint Task Force; Director National Cyber-Forensics and Training Alliance; Director Strategic Alliance Cyber Crime Working Group; Director Coordinated Cyber Action Teams; Director CIA CTC [Counter Terror Center] Cyber-Terror Division; DUSCYBERCOM; DSEC Enforcement Division.
Re: Response to attack on U.S. financial system

P resident Willets had already heard most of what the assembled experts in counter cyber-terrorism were going to say because DFBI Grant Wallace had kept him abreast of developments throughout the day yesterday. The president nodded to Director Wallace to start the emergency meeting.

"Thank you, Mr. President. You are all, no doubt, aware that our financial systems are under attack. The exchanges are slated to open in two hours, and one example of the status of the systems should suffice: The Dow Industrial was at an all-time high three days ago—19,231. The Dow will open at 4,182 this morning. Our country as lost nearly $800 billion to this point in time, and the market remains in free fall."

There was a small shared gasp in the room.

"Obviously, this cannot go on. There is no doubt that it is a deliberate and well-coordinated assault on the United States and could not have come at a worse time, given the precarious status of our economy vis-à-vis the national debt. Since the attack was discovered yesterday morning, we have thrown every cyber asset—government, military, and private—into the investigation. The FBI, CIA, USCYBERCOM, Homeland Security, General Motors, Delta Airlines and their cyber protection group, the SEC, and the United Banking Cyber Coalition are all involved.

"We are all but certain that the Russians are behind it, but we could never prove it in a court of law. We do know for certain that the Russian Mafia is involved because we have found signatures embedded in the hacking worms in our computer systems which are known to be the mark of two infamous Russian teen-age hackers, Afanasy Fedoseev and Lyosha Demidov. Although we have no such direct evidence, we can always be sure that the daughter of the head of one of the largest *russkaya mafiya* organizations, Renata Leonidovna Zaslavsky, is in the thick of it."

"Well, that could not be more ticklish," Secretary of State Thompson Kennedy said, "a public accusation against the Tikhondnko regime would be such an insult that the Russians would be duty bound to strike back. They are crude, and their strike would probably be a military one, and one to which we would be honor bound to reciprocate. We need to be creative and to tread lightly."

President Willets agreed, "We are in no position to give in to a scenario that includes military adventurism. However, Director Wallace is also correct; this assault will cripple us— probably permanently—and cannot be allowed to go entirely unanswered. Unfortunately, for us, we do not have any kind of grace period during which diplomatic endeavors can be of any significant benefit."

Secretary Kennedy had more to add, but decided to wait until a later point in the discussion to say his piece.

"Let's hear your ideas, ladies and gentlemen," President Willets asked.

"I think we have what may be an acceptable answer—one which cuts right to the chase," DCIA Andrew Dillon said.

Director Dillon was chronically ill with congestive heart disease and was nearing the end of a one-year courtesy stint as DCIA as a reward for his forty years of service to The Company. He was tired and no longer felt that he had the strength to tackle such horrendous problems as the one currently under consideration. He knew that President Willets had chosen his successor and that it would probably be the current Surgeon General who was also a high-ranking special agent of the CIA. It could not happen soon enough for his liking.

"We have a special agent who holds an Ultra SCI [Top-Secret, Sensitive Compartmentalized Information, i.e. "above Top Secret"] clearance rating with SSBI [Single Scope Background Investigation rating. The president has authorized me to tell you the agent's name because she is almost certainly going to be my successor, and he will need your help to get her confirmed because her accomplishments cannot be made public. She is Dr. Sybil Norcroft."

In a day of striking revelations, that one ranked right up there with the rest. For most of the attendees, Sybil's involvement with the CIA was a revelation; and that she was of such a rank within the Company that she would be considered for the position of director was nothing short of a shock.

Dillon continued without allowing discussion of his revelation; so, he could go on to an even more sensational one.

"Some time ago, she planted software from a USB device into the Russian president's own computer and also into the SVR computer system. That software enables us not only to get every scintilla of information that passes among the administration, the intelligence community, and the military; but also allows us at the push of a button to interfere with almost any computer based function in the country. I will spare you the details of the intruder; but, trust me when I tell you that we can stop trains, cut off sections or the entire electrical grid, scramble air controller signals, confuse electronic signaling throughout the Russian Federation—you name it. And the best thing about it is that we can do any or all of that without leaving evidence that it was us. Until now, we have allowed our worm to lie silent in their supercomputer systems."

The DUSCYBERCOM [Director U.S. Cyber Command], Cyril Farnsworth, asked, "What are our risks if we use the CIA's worm?"

"Miniscule. Unlike the historical Stuxnet computer worm, there is no possible boomerang effect. There are no embedded vanity signatures. None of the interruptions can be traced to U.S. sources."

"I'm going to shorten this discussion and cut right to the chase," the president said, "several of you here have suggested that we contact President Tikhondnko and Prime Minister Yudin forthwith and make a threat or two. There doesn't seem to be any quick way to deal with Leonid Aleksandrovich Zaslavsky, the *vory v zakone* [syndicate boss and chief of the thieves-in-law] of the *Solntsevskaya Bratva, russkaya mafiya* [Russian mafia] who is likely the real culprit in all of this. I am hoping that we can persuade Tikhondnko to handle them."

"If he can," Secretary Wallace said.

"It is better than war, which seems like the only other option. They have fired the first salvo, and a cybertage assault in kind would seem to be a measured response. A threat would be a much softer approach, but I am afraid the Russians are more the 'show-me' kind of people than the 'tell-me' kind."

There was a unanimous vote by those present to have President Willets brave the bear in his cave.

Chapter Six

"Mr. President, it's the red phone," the executive secretary said.

Calls on the red phone could only be from the American President, the Chairman of the Communist Party of the PRC, or the Director-General of the United Nations.

"It is the U.S. president, Sir."

"Hello, Parker. To what do I owe this pleasure?"

"As you might expect, the use of this telephone means I am not calling for a frivolous bit of chit-chat."

"Indeed so."

"I will come directly to the point."

"You always do. That is one thing I like about you, Parker."

"And I, you, Afonasii Glebovich. You cannot be unaware of our financial problems."

"Of course not, my friend. You have our sincerest sympathy, and I extend my hand in an offer of help. How can I assist you? We have not forgotten your assistance during our Era of Stagnation while we were experimenting with collective rule."

"Afonsaii Glebovich, our current financial woes are serious; they are the result of a deliberate attack on our financial infrastructure; and they have been traced back to the Russian government as identified by our financial, counter cyber terrorism, and law enforcement agencies. My government and I personally, are deeply offended by your country's actions. As one leader of reform a super-power to another, I am giving you the courtesy of a personal call to ask you to correct this dangerous path."

"And, I am affronted by your accusation. How dare you, Sir!? We have done nothing of the kind. I demand that you send us your so-called 'evidence' so that we can evaluate its validity. You are treading on dangerous ground yourself if you think you can make such a challenge to the great Russian nation with impunity!"

"I see that courtesy and diplomacy are not going to carry the day, President Tikhondnko. This is what we expect to happen. By this afternoon at the latest, the short-selling attack on our stock market will cease; the perpetrators who are not already in our custody will be identified by you and turned over to us; and you will force Zaslavsky and his *Solntsevskaya Bratva* to cease and desist from his cyber and trading assaults on our financial institutions."

"Or what? You will stamp your foot or pound on your U.N. desk to show your anger and frustration? Do you think we are naughty children whom you can make cower with a threat?"

"No, Sir. I think none of that. I believe you are the ultimate pragmatists and learn effectively from objective demonstrations. I will bid you good-bye, Afonasii Glebovich; and I will await your call."

President Willets hung up his end of the line.

President Tikhondnko shouted a string of obscenities before calming down enough to think rationally.

"*They cannot afford a war. They have no evidence to use against us on the world stage. They are posturing. If they have something in mind, we will wait to see what it is and act accordingly. Who does that pipsqueak think he is giving the President of All the Russias orders?*"

President Willets called the DCIA on his secure personal line.

"This is NI One [The designation of POTUS as the commander-in-chief of the intelligence services as well as of the armed forces of the United States]. Andrew, please initiate the first phase of the cyber intervention."

"Yes, Sir. It will be done."

Fifteen minutes later, President Tikhondnko received an urgent conference call from Colonel General Yevgeni Mitrokhin, Director of the SVR [Foreign Intelligence Service], Michael Levinovich Ledvinov, Director of the MVD [Ministry of Internal Affairs], and General Ivan Petrovsky-Yugantsev, Supreme Commander-in-Chief of the Armed Forces of the Russian Federation.

Gen. Petrovsky-Yugantsev was the spokesman, "Comrade Chairman, we have been the victim of an extremely potent cyber-attack. Our electronic communications systems are all nonfunctional. We are calling you from the Old Veterans Club in central Moscow because our secure official lines do not work. We cannot prove it, but either the Chinese or the Americans are responsible. We are trying to identify which but without success as yet. Shall we launch a counter attack; and if so, at whom?"

"Do nothing and be patient for now. I am quite certain who did this. Let us wait a bit and learn."

Fifteen minutes after that, the lesson was intensified. Every financial apparatchik in Tikhondnko's administration called the president's office. The reports were all the same: "We have had a complete melt-down of our computer system."

Tikhondnko sighed and arranged for a call on the red phone. To his fury, he was informed that the President of the United States was busy on another call on that line and would he please hold until the president could get back to him.

"I hold for no man," Tikhondnko screamed and slammed down his receiver.

On the other end, the red phone was indeed busy. President Willets was talking to PRC Chairman Liew Bao-Zhi in Beijing.

"Thank you for taking my call, Mr. Chairman. As you no doubt are already informed, I am calling about a serious matter and wish to ask your further help. My nation is grateful for what you have already done for us. Our problems have escalated and now we have fairly concrete evidence that our financial systems have been compromised—more accurately, attacked—by elements of the Russian Federation, and our stock markets are in free fall. We estimate our losses to be nearly a trillion U.S. dollars, and there is no end in sight. This attack—of course—affects you and your investments in the United States as well. We have taken countermeasures which we believe will be effective, but before we can improve our current condition, we are going to need a massive infusion of cash."

"I believe such an amount would be most difficult for us to add to your already extraordinary indebtedness to us, Mr. President. We simply cannot extend further credit, despite my truly genuine desire to help."

"I believe we can reach an accommodation, Chairman Liew. What I propose is that you begin the process of transferring funds to our financial trading institutions, and I will arrange today to have a full trillion dollars plus 10% interest in gold bullion transferred from Fort Knox before the close of business today. Can we operate from a relationship of trust, my friend?"

"We can. As soon as we hang up, I will make the cash flow from our end."

"And I will begin filling the Chinese ship of your choice with gold bullion as soon as I am off the line."

"Done," Chairman Liew said.

President Willets chose not to call the Russian president back. Instead he called Treasury Secretary Richard Pennyweight.

"Richard,"

"Yes, Mr. President?"

"Begin immediately to transfer the gold bullion to the Chinese freighter. Chairman Liew's office will call you shortly to let you know the correct ship. The shipment must get underway today. I know that such a movement of funds will attract public interest because of the huge army security force that will have to accompany it, but try and keep as much of the transaction as secret as you can."

"Yes, Sir. I will make it happen."

President Tikhondnko received two more disturbing calls. The first was from Colonel General Mitrokhin, Director of the SVR.

"Comrade President, you need to know that the Chinese have made a wire transfer of a trillion U.S. dollars to shore up the falling stock markets there. In addition, almost every agent of Zaslavsky's in the U.S. has been rounded up; and for all practical purposes, the attack on the U.S. financial institutions has failed and is over."

"Thank you, Comrade General."

The second call came a minute later. It was from the mayor of Moscow.

"Mr. President, I have learned from the security forces that the armed forces' computer systems are shut down. A minute ago, our street light computer control system went completely berserk. It is beyond chaos in the inner city; it's mayhem. What can be done about this catastrophe?"

"I will deal with it, Mayor Rasniski."

Tikhondnko swallowed his pride and had his secretary call on the red phone one more time.

"I regret to inform you that there will be a short delay before the president can take your call, Mr. President. He has asked me to inform you that he is dealing with a national security issue which should be brief, and he will be back with you in a very few minutes. He asked that you hold for him."

Tikhondnko resigned himself to the idea that the U.S. had gained the upper hand; and he would have to be patient; and worse, he would have to ask for a cessation of the escalating hostilities before the two superpowers began shooting real bullets.

President Willets was on the line with the Secretary of the Treasury and with the DCIA discussing the news of the Chinese infusion of cash and the fact that their cyber-attack on Russia was having a desirable affect. He congratulated his subordinates on their prompt responses then had his secretary get him on the line with Tikhondnko.

"I am sorry to keep you waiting, Afonasii Glebovich. It was truly unavoidable under the very trying circumstances I am facing. What is it that I can do for you?"

"I believe it has come down to what can each of us do for the other," President Tikhondnko said, straining to keep his voice calm and his communication civil.

"You called me, Mr. President. Perhaps you should take the lead."

"I suppose that would be best. We admit nothing; but in the interest of our continuing cordial national relations, I will see what I can do about correcting whatever the criminal organizations in our country are up to. Will you terminate your cybertage before things escalate out of control?"

"I am not aware of any kind of cybertage against your great nation, Afonasii Glebovich; but, like you, I will do my best to see if such an outrage is emanating from my country. We certainly do not want further aggressive agendas to be implemented. As we make progress, it would be best for us to call each other again with a progress report once we have been able complete an emergency investigation. Please let me know what comes of your communication with Zaslavsky."

Tikhondnko seethed at the presumption of the American president, but knew that he was dead-on accurate; so, he made no protest. As soon as the two presidents finished there call, he had his secretary contact Leonid Zaslavsky at his home office on Paradise Ponds.

"Mr. President, to what do I owe this honor?" the crime syndicate czar answered.

"There's no time for informalities, Leonid. The U.S. has responded to an intolerable degree against your adventurism towards their financial markets. They have—for all practical purposes—shut down the military, the government, and the communications and transportation systems of our country. President Willets has informed me that they can do more. We really do not want more. It is not in our interests to continue to turn a blind eye and a deaf ear to your attacks in the U.S. You will do that because it is in the best interest of your organization to do so; and it is in our mutual best interest not to have this matter escalate between us."

Zaslavsky was not used to being threatened by anyone, not even the president of all the Russias; but he was a practical man; so, his reply was conciliatory.

"All right, Mr. President, because you have had the courtesy to call me personally and to avoid casting blame, I will make the current activities of the *Solntsevskaya Bratva* cease. You have my word."

"Thank you friend, Leonid. I trust that this mutual agreement between us will allow us to deal with each other in a mutually beneficial fashion in the future."

After he and the president disconnected from each other, Zaslavsky said to himself with gritted teeth, "*Those arrogant Americans have not heard the last of this. They will regret the day they disrespected the Solntsevskaya Bratva.*"

He sent for Ivan Droskovsky who had a special skill set that he needed.

Chapter Seven

John Burr Physical Education Building, Advanced Judo Course [PHED 015], Howard University, Washington D.C., November 30, 2019

Cerisse Daniels enjoyed physical contact sports, and was very much at home in the John Burr gymnasium. On the upper floor was her home away from home—the judo room. The sport—known by its originators as "the gentle way" was perfect for her because her diminutive size was not a significant factor. That she was nimble, agile, quick, and smart gave her an advantage over many much larger opponents, including males. She had earned respect in the judo room; and because the sport was not particularly popular, the room was often vacant. Cerisse liked the quiet, the familiar smells, and the opportunity to be alone to study. Well—of course—she was never alone. When she started her freshman year at Howard, she had the constant companionship of two secret service agents assigned to her by a presidential order because her mother, Dr. Sybil Norcroft

Daniels, was the Surgeon General and was a woman who generated controversy as she went about working to improve and to protect the health of Americans. During the past two weeks—because of an increased threat level coming from the recent cyber-attacks launched by the Russians on the nation's financial institutions—President Willets increased the Secret Service unit assigned to Cerisse to four men and women; so, she could have at least three protectors at all times.

Having the watchers was a drag for Cerisse. She had enough baggage anyway without having four big brutes hovering around her all of the time. Her very small size, very black skin, and her very high-profile mother, made her stand out like a neon light in a dark room wherever she went. At least, that is what she thought. Today, she was less than her usual sunny self. Her left arm pit hurt—annoying, not really serious—because her mother, the Surgeon General had required her to have a GPS tracking card inserted subcutaneously in her armpit; so, she could be located if anyone kidnapped her, as if anyone would be really interested in anyone as obscure and unimportant as she was. She realized that her self-concepts were inconsistent, almost schizophrenic; and that was part of why she felt out of sorts. What she needed was a fight. She needed to see her boyfriend, Drake. She knew that what she really needed was to get back to work studying for her calculus final, and she was out of sorts about that, too.

This was a mid-day watch for her Secret Service minders; so, all four of them were on guard. Two of them were pretending to be invisible in the judo room with her, and the other two were pretending to blend in with the crowds milling about on the campus between Greene Stadium, Burr Gymnasium, Cook Hall, and Drew Hall. There were several difficulties associated with that effort: there were very few students out and about that afternoon; the agents were huge, powerful looking men in contrast to the average size of and age of the students; the agents were Caucasian—something like the Aryan hordes—whereas, more than 90% of the students and faculty passing by them were African-American; they were all dressed in casual student attire that made them look as phony as a three-dollar bill.

Someone was watching the watchers. A team of six people—a mix of male and female, Asian, Negroid, and Eastern European—mingled with the few students out-and-about that cold winter's afternoon. They were very much aware of the Secret Service watchers, but the U.S. agents were not aware of them. The six person team knew exactly where little Cerisse Daniels was inside Burr Gymnasium.

Oval Office, The White House, Washington D.C., December 12, 2019, 0730 hrs
Present: POTUS, VPOTUS, DCIA, DDCIA, SURGEON GENERAL
Re: Appointment of a new DCIA

Vice-President Tanner L. Oldroyd, CIA Director Andrew Dillon, DDCIA Porter Farnsworth, and Surgeon General Sybil Norcroft, M.D., Ph.D., F.A.C.S. sat in the comfortable arm chairs and love seat facing the president who was smiling. A steward silently brought in a platter of steaming demitasse cups of an exotic aromatic Asian tea and small breakfast croissants then left just as unobtrusively.

"It's early, I know, my friends; but I am going to have a very busy day today. Thanks for getting up and braving the storm to meet with me at this painful hour," President Willets said. "I have an announcement, and I want you all to be witnesses. This is something of an historic occasion. Without further ado, it is my privilege to appoint our own esteemed colleague, Dr. Norcroft, as the new Director of the Central Intelligence Agency. She will replace Andrew Dillon who has given more than forty years of his life to the Agency and has contributed immeasurably to the safety and security of America. I wanted to congratulate Sybil and to give a heartfelt private thank you to Andrew for a job well done. The public announcements will come this evening at a photo-op in the East Room. This appointment is indeed historical; Dr. Norcroft will break another glass ceiling by becoming the first female Director of the Central Intelligence Agency of the United States.

"Because of several recent and ongoing situations—the furor over the austerity measures, the nastiness of the Russian attempt to undermine our financial institutions, and the reaction of the Chinese conservatives to Chairman Liew's generous help during our financial crisis—I have issued a new—or more accurately, a renewed—presidential order authorizing the Secret Service to provide upgraded security for a number of our top officials and their families, including all present. I realize that it is annoying to have the security details around all of the time; but the FBI is adamant that there is a high-level of threat for attack, kidnapping, and terrorism now. Thank you for your indulgence."

When the president concluded his brief remarks, the four officers in the Oval Office applauded each other and the president. None of them disagreed with his choices, and all of them recognized that they had their work cut out to get Sybil through the Senate Advise and Consent process since her real past contributions to the espionage world had to remain top secret. The skids had been greased by the administration to ensure smooth passage by giving all of the senior senators a briefing in which President Willets pledged his personal word that Sybil was the woman for the job; not only did she deserve it; but her contributions up to this point—the secret ones—made her a necessary cog in the intelligence world's wheels.

Conference Room, Office of the Secretary, U.S. Department of Health & Human Services, 200 Independence Avenue, S.W., Washington D.C., December 13, 2019, 1015 hrs

Secretary Margoles invited Dr. Norcroft to his office; so, she could officially bow out of the government's efforts to establish a National Health Service in time to avert bankruptcy by the American republic. Frank Margoles was frankly miffed at the president and at Sybil for making that choice—changing horses in the middle of the stream. It was not personal; he liked Sybil, respected her, and valued her contributions.

"Oh, Sybil, why hast thou forsaken me?" he said as soon as she took her seat in the spacious office.

"It was a hard decision, Frank; I assure you. Medicine has always been my first love and has dominated my life since I entered college as a freshman. For reasons I can't discuss, the president wants me to head up the CIA; and it was not a request I could lightly refuse. I'm sure you have more than an inkling of the pressures involved."

"Of course I do, Sybil; but I don't have to like it. Getting down to business, I appreciate the research you have been doing, and I hope the new Surgeon General will be able to capture the vision to the degree you have. I'll buzz in the rest and let you bring us up to speed."

Margoles tapped a button on his desk top, and his office assistant ushered nine HHS officers into the conference room. The division heads of the AoA [Administration on Aging], ACF [Administration for Children and Families], AHRQ [Agency for Health Care Research and Quality], FDA [Food and Drug Administration], CMS [Centers for Medicare and Medicaid Services], HRSA [Health Resources and Services Administration], IHS [Indian Health Services], NIH [National Institutes of Health], and SAMHSA [Substance Abuse and Mental Health Services Administration] took their seats and opened the folders Drs. Margoles and Norcroft had prepared for them.

Secretary Margoles said, "I presume Gen. Norcroft does not need to be introduced; so, we will hear her parting words for us on the question of establishing a National Health Service."

Sybil immediately caught the attention of the HHS brain trust by greeting each of them by name.

"Thanks for being willing to hear my last hurrah. I suppose that this is my last act as a medical doctor, and it is a bitter-sweet day for me. All of us face a daunting task with all of its political, religious, tradition-bound, economic, social, and philosophical ramifications. But, please keep in mind that—absent real health care reform—18% and an increasing percentage of the GDP will be caused by medical care alone. That percentage could climb to 20—25—maybe even 30% by 2030 and 35-40% by 2040 which is unsustainable by itself, to say nothing of our ever upward spiraling national debt. To put it into perspective for the average middle-class family—especially households with employer-sponsored health insurance—this trend indicates that a rapidly progressive smaller fraction of their total compensation will be in the form of take-home pay and a progressively larger fraction will take the form of employer-provided health insurance. That is, if employers remain willing to provide employee benefits which is by no means a certainty.

"The first thirty pages in your folder are the third quarter report from the Congressional Joint Economy Committee.

There you will find the most up-to-date information available, and you will promptly recognize why the report has been held back from the general public. You can peruse the data at your leisure, and I do suggest strongly that you digest it. This information will form the basis of your talking points as you spread out to spread the 'gospel' of National Health Service. This information should convince you that the need is inescapable."

The folder held information on the third quarter gross domestic product, income, employment, production, business activity, prices, money, credit, security markets, Federal finance, health care spreadsheet, and international statistics—including health care comparisons among the G-12 nations. The folder had consumed most of Sybil's time in her office during her tenure as the Surgeon General, and she was justifiably proud of her work and was willing to give strong support to her conclusions.

"The economy is improving, but not to the extent necessary to permit us to pay down on our national indebtedness; we are on the brink of being unable to pay the interest, as you well know. Our saving grace is that the Chinese have floated us yet another loan—one with serious fiduciary requirements. The problem is that the jobs being created do not pay enough to have our middle-class contribute sufficiently in taxes to allow us to get control of our indebtedness. Not with our current rate of spending. And the biggest culprit in the equation is medical care delivery.

"The CEA [Council of Economic Advisers] has undertaken a comprehensive analysis of the economic impacts of health care reform since 2010 when the PPACA was signed into law. In your folder there is an overview of current and projected economic impacts of health care in the United States and a forecast of where we would be headed in the absence of reform. Unfortunately, the flaws of the PPACA—mainly the result of the partisan political animus which surrounded its enactment—cancelled out its well-intentioned benefits. That does not change the facts of the critical need for health-care reform—the inefficiencies, market failures, waste, and greed—prior to 2010 and which still persist in the current health care system. The fundamentals are still there, and we will have a limited discussion of the key components of health care.

We will conclude with an analysis of the economic effects of slowing health care cost growth and expanding coverage—which were the principle aims of the PPACA. The faults of U.S. health care delivery are myriad, and the blame can be spread far and wide. We must learn from the failures that became so blaringly apparent in late fall 2013, stop playing politics, and start the repair. All of that will take a radical departure from the status quo, and there will be a great many important toes that get stepped on. That cannot dissuade you; the answer is a single-party payer under the control of the United States government—a National Health Service.

"The CEA report reveals large economic impacts of genuine health care reform, not just good intentions or party rhetoric. Even a modest 1.5% slowing of the rate of health care costs would increase the real GDP by 2% in two years from now and up to nearly 8% ten years from now. That is a start and not good enough, but it is real. That would increase the income of a typical family of four by $2,600 in 2022 and $10,000 in 2030. That degree of slowing cost growth would lower our unemployment rate to a point consistent with steady inflation by improving our situation by approximately one-quarter of a percentage point. The CEA's estimate of beneficial impact on employment rates is that—in the short and medium run—it is estimated to be approximately 500,000 new jobs *each year* that the effect is felt.

"Furthermore, expanding health insurance coverage to the uninsured—to decrease dramatically the number of so-called 'free-riders' would increase net economic well-being of the United States by roughly $100 billion a year or 0.67%—two-thirds of a percent—of GDP. Real reform would likely increase labor supply, decrease our dependence on illegal foreign labor, remove unnecessary barriers to job mobility, and help to equalize the small business versus large business discrepancies which put small businesses—the backbone of the middle-class—at such a disadvantage.

The progressive aging of our population is a factor that must be reckoned with since aging adds an additional one-quarter to the GDP percentage consumed by health care. There is no question that even that small savings would go a long way towards preventing disastrous increases in the federal budget deficit if we had the time. Unfortunately, we do not have the time. We have at an absolute maximum two years; so, our timetable must be quickly put into high gear.

"Despite every effort by the Obama and subsequent administrations, there are still 45 million Americans without health care insurance; and they remain a prominent drain on our economy and siphon off money from the pockets of those who have insurance. The percentage of free-riders will continue to increase, according to CEA projections—consider what 72-75 million uninsured would do to our economy by 2040. That is a very real projection largely based on the rate of small businesses being unable or unwilling to provide healthcare insurance to their employees. Inefficiencies, rewarding medical inputs—fee-for-service—waste, inappropriately high administrative costs, incompetency in focusing on cure rather than prevention, fraud, and defensive medicine take a huge toll, and the impact worsens every year. In a sense, none of that will matter in three or four years, because we will be bankrupt; and only the very rich will be able to afford good medical care. Much of that care will be obtained outside the borders of the United States."

Sybil paused to sip some water.

"So, Madam Surgeon General, we are all pretty much aware of the downside of our current failing system and of our responsibility to educate the public about that, but what can we do about it? I mean, what would a National Health Service do?"

"Excellent question. Americans are justifiably dubious about the role of government in medical care because—for one thing—they point to the many and obvious inefficiencies in government already present, many of which are related to political patronage issues. It will be necessary to return to basics and to have a board of managers which is impervious to political influence and is monitored regularly to ensure against bribery, undue influence, and graft. A dedicated law enforcement agency to investigate, arrest, prosecute, and try the managers and their employees for malfeasance will be a necessity. The board will have to operate under a mandate to control costs. That will involve real and objective scrutiny of practices, procedures, devices, drugs, and inefficiencies.

Outcomes must be clearly defined and based on verifiable evidence rather than on popularity or deep-seated personal beliefs on the part of care givers or patients. We must not be the first to try something new nor the last to abandon an old and established practice. That will be an ongoing study, and will take courage on the part of the managers to stand up to drug and device manufacturers, established medical groups, litigation attorneys, and representatives of the public including—dare I say—minorities.

"The system must be simple, clear, and understandable by even relatively undereducated people. There must be compassionate, firm, and well-informed help available. Electronic record keeping and communications among patients and their care givers and with other providers must become routine. We do not need to do even a quarter of the cardiac procedures that we currently do. Spine surgeons do not need to do fusions with the implantation of ghastly expensive hardware in anywhere near as many patients with back pain. Hysterectomies as stand-alone operations should be largely abandoned in favor of much less expensive and efficient robotic procedures to include re-attaching the structures involved in pelvic prolapse, despite the upfront costs of the machinery. Tort reform is critical.

Those are just a few of the examples of cost cutting combined with superior evidence-based performance requirements that must be implemented in the National Health Service law and will reduce costs and increase performance drastically, which is the result we must have. Every single individual in the country must have health insurance; and those who are able must pay for it. We must make it less difficult for healthy people to receive actuarially reasonable rates.

"As Jesus said, 'the poor will always be with us,' and we will always have to factor in the costs of care for them. What we have now is disastrously expensive, and even an increased humanitarian contribution will be less costly. We must do all of this within weeks, not years. It is time posthumous that we did away with the fiddle-faddle which has consumed our efforts at healthcare delivery reform over the past nearly ten years. The people must be educated; the brain trust of the government and our universities must go into high gear; the Congress must act; and finally, the implementation program must be fully ready before a date certain of the switch over to a National Health Service is announced. We will not survive another debacle like the one that took place when the Obama PPACA was pronounced ready for patient participation.

"Ladies and gentlemen, my friends and fellow Americans, I thank you for the privilege I have been given to serve with you. In this and all of your endeavors, I wish you fair winds and a following sea. In the final analysis, I wish you success. As NASA control radioed back to Apollo 13 when things were going horribly wrong, and it appeared that three very good men were going to die, 'failure is not an option'."

Chapter Eight

This was to have been Cerisse's first New Year's Eve away from home since she was adopted by Charles and Sybil Daniels five years ago. However, she relented and persuaded her boyfriend, Drake Farrer, to come to the house for dinner and to get to know her parents better. He compromised with her that they could go out after dinner to the Howard Science Students' New Year's bash. She liked it that he was willing to accommodate her, and he was strong enough to wrest a compromise from her. She pretty much liked everything he did.

After dinner, Charles Daniels invited Drake to come into his study; so, they could talk. It was so provincial that Drake and Cerisse shared an amused little laugh, but kept her parents from seeing their mirth.

"Have a seat and relax, Drake. This is not the fuddy-duddy old father having *that* conversation with his precious daughter's new boyfriend. On the contrary, Cerisse's mother and

I are pleased with how the two of you are getting on. From everything we can learn, you are a fine upstanding man with a bright future. It's that future we'd like to discuss with you. So that I don't make unwarranted presumptions, would it be all right if I asked you a few questions?"

"Of course, Sir."

"To start off, I think 'Sir' is too stuffy. Would you mind just calling me 'Mr. Daniels' and calling Sybil's mom—her Mama—Dr. Norcroft. The Daniels part came after she got her M.D., and so the doctor goes with Norcroft rather than Daniels to be technical about it."

"Sure."

"I hope you are okay with me calling you by your first name."

"I prefer it."

"Great. Now to the questions. This is not a grilling, nor do you have to feel obligated to answer anything. If you are unsure, a simple, 'I don't know' will suffice."

Drake nodded.

"Are you and Cerisse serious? Are you exclusive with each other?"

"Yes to both questions, Mr. Daniels."

"I'm glad to hear it. I guess that leads to the next things I would like to know. What are your plans for your future education and how do they include Cerisse?"

"That's something of a tough one, Mr. Daniels. If it were a perfect world, I would like for us to get married at the end of this school year. We'll both be twenty at that time. I'll be frank with you and answer a question you have been too polite to ask. We have not had intimate relations with each other. I am crazy with desire for her, and I think she feels the same way about me. We want to be virgins when we get married; but we are only human; and we can't wait a whole lot longer. Therein lies the rub. My family is not at all well-to-do. We are comfortable. I work outside school, but I can't afford to get married and finish my undergrad work and get into medical school. At best that would bog Cerisse and me down with debt before we ever got started and would probably derail my education and also hers. We are planning to have a serious talk this week about what we are going to do. We are on the horns of a dilemma."

"Drake, you said that you and Cerisse want to remain virgins until you are married. I applaud that. But I have to ask an indelicate question. Are you aware of our little girl's childhood in the Congo?"

"Mr. Daniels, I am aware of everything. Cerisse stopped me from having even another date after it began to look serious for us. She told me that she had to tell me something and that she would understand if I didn't want to have anything more to do with her. I was kind of stunned, but told her that nothing but her happiness mattered to me. Then, she poured it all out. I understand that I am the only person other than the two of you she has ever told."

"How did you react, Drake? That had to have been a shocker."

"It was. It might sound silly or girlish to you, but I cried. She looked into my face to see what my tears meant, and it was clear that they were an expression of my sympathy, my deep hurt that she had been so maltreated. She cried too. I told her that none of it—none of it—mattered. None of it was her fault. She is a virgin to me. That was really important to her, and I would never violate her in the slightest degree now that we have shared such a profound secret and pain."

He looked directly into Charles's eyes.

Charles shed a few tears. He had no further questions for Drake. The young man had won him over completely.

Cerisse and her parents would be privileged to have a man of Drake Farrer's depth of character to be Cerisse's husband.

"Drake, it has to be obvious to you that Sybil and I accept you whole heartedly. We could not have asked for a better man for our precious little girl. She has been through a lot; she is tough and resilient; but there is a tender core in the girl. If you nurture that core, she will be the best wife a young doctor could ask for. If you treat her well, I will do all in my power to help you realize your dreams, if you will let me."

"I'm not sure what you're saying, Mr. Daniels. I do very much appreciate your wholehearted acceptance of me and of Cerisse and my intentions—as murky as they are— for the moment."

"I would like to clarify some of that murkiness. I know something of what it takes to be a doctor, especially to become a neurosurgeon. The hurdles will be all that much greater with both of you getting your educations. I would like to make you an offer."

"Yes, Mr. Daniels?"

"I understand and appreciate your passion and your dilemma. Of course Mrs. Daniels and I will always think our little child is too young to get married, but we can be objective enough to learn differently. If the two of you decide that marriage is the best thing for you, and money seems to be the only major hurdle, then I would like to help you get through your educations—no strings attached."

"Like a loan?"

"No, think of it as a wedding gift—one that keeps on giving. When you become rich doctors, you can take care of the doddering old folks at home."

"I don't know what to say. That is the most incredible piece of luck in my entire life."

"There is no such thing as luck, Drake. I compete in a dog-eat-dog business world and have done so for a long time. You have earned my offer. I ask only that you continue to earn it."

"I will take care of Cerisse all the days of my life. I will protect her, love her, and make her as happy as it is possible to be. Your offer is life to me. I will owe you forever. Thank you so much."

They shook hands on the most important bargain two men can make.

While the two men were in the study having their talk, Sybil took Cerisse aside in the sitting room outside hers and Charles's bed room.

"I know what Daddy is doing, Mama; I just hope he isn't too old-fashioned and stodgy with Drake."

"You know your daddy better than that, Cerisse. I will bet you a milkshake that they come out of that room all smiles."

"I certainly hope so."

"There's something else I need to talk to you about alone. You know about my new job."

"Of course, Mama, everybody in the country—probably in the world—knows that you are the new director of the CIA."

"Yes. You have to understand that we are in very unsettling times. What you might not know is that I have been receiving lots of threats lately, ever since the impeachment proceedings. I am not popular because of my participation in the imposition of martial law three years ago. Now, there are a lot of people who threaten me and my family because of the new efforts to stave off national bankruptcy, especially my role in pushing forward a plan to start a National Health Service."

"But, you're out of that, right? How come Secretary Margoles and the people in the SEC and the Medicare and Medicaid agencies testified before the congressional committee that it was all the president's and your ideas. They got scared and blamed you, right? I thought they were your friends."

"Cerisse, my dear, there's a saying that has a lot of truth to it—'in Washington, if you need a friend, get a dog'. That's cynical but seems accurate."

"It's not fair, and it's nasty."

Sybil nodded.

"The people who are blaming me are just covering themselves. They will continue to work for the National Health Service and probably to blame me. I don't really care so long as they do their jobs and get the nation's health care delivery back on track. I am no longer actively involved; but the hatred and threats from the radical right-wing people have not let up. You recognize that our security guard unit has doubled in size and that we have to obey some rules about where and when we can go out and with whom. Incidentally, presuming that you intend to keep company with Drake, he will have to have his own guards. The president has signed a special order to provide our whole family—including Drake—with a very serious security force. I have got to trust you to comply with the requests—yes, the orders—of the Secret Service agents. Will you do that for me?"

"Yes, Mama. I won't like it, but I understand that it is necessary. Will things ever get better?"

"Frankly, Cerisse, I don't think they will until I complete my term—which is indefinite—as the DCIA. I am going to tell you a family secret. You are an adult, and a very intelligent and serious one. There have been threats from the Russians against me and a lot of other U.S. officials because of some financial crimes they tried to get away with."

"From the Russian government?"

"Certainly not directly, but there have been very direct ones from the Russian mafia who want to extort concessions from our government to let them have a free rein to invest in our stock markets. They will destroy us if we let them do it, and all of us in the federal government are absolute in our opposition to them. That is probably as important a reason as any to have the security units protect us. I repeat; will you do what I ask and what your guardians tell you without making it difficult?"

"I will, Mama. I swear on my love for you that I will."

Chapter Nine

House No. 6, Maly Patriarshy Pereulok, South-west Side of Patriarshiye Ponds, Moscow, Home of Leonid Aleksandrovich Zaslavsky, the *vory v zakone* [syndicate boss and chief of the thieves-in-law] of the *Solntsevskaya Bratva, russkaya mafiya* [Russian mafia], January 7, 2020, 0900 hrs

Leonid Aleksandrovich's assistant handed him the telephone receiver.

"I have Droskovsky on the line Mr. Zaslavsky."

"Droskovsky, tell me what you have."

"We have four accessible targets. The mission can be accomplished."

"Safely?"

"We can get the packages into our control, and we can get them back to the ponds. We will likely meet resistance, and there is a high probability that there will be some unpleasantness."

"That is to be expected. No harm can come to the packages. That is an absolute, Ivan Vladimirovich."

"Understood. I cannot say the same for the security people or for my own people, for that matter."

"Collateral damage can't be avoided. We knew that from the beginning. Proceed."

"It will be done, Mr. Zaslavsky. I will inform you when we are back in the Rodin and near the ponds."

John Burr Physical Education Building, Judo Room, Howard University, Washington D.C., January 11, 2020, 2200 hrs

Cerisse had an hour long Friday evening workout with Drake and one of her Secret Service guards, a wiry martial arts expert named Calandra Davenport. She was small, but still more than a head taller than Cerisse. The two women had become fast friends and nearly equal competitors on the judo mat. Drake was much larger than both of them but no match for either of the small women. Besides Cerisse and Drake, there was a full contingent of Secret Service security agents in the room who were bored stiff. That included one nominally assigned exclusively to Drake Farrer. Most agents hated being on security details protecting people who were very unlikely targets. There was nothing to alleviate the boredom because they had to be ready at a second's notice to spring into action. After days, weeks, and months of watching over little Cerisse Daniels, the agents were only dimly aware that they had lost their edge. Two of the men were fighting sleep and dreading having to sit outside her dorm room door for the rest of the night trying to stay awake.

The competitors were stretched out on the floor. Calandra's weapons were lying ten feet away just off the mat. Cerisse and Drake were lying supine on the floor holding hands as their pulse and respiratory rates slowly calmed down. Cerisse was aware of the strong smell of sweat coming from Drake, Calandra, and herself. She rather liked the aroma because it evoked feelings of strength, health, and vigor. Her ghetto blaster was playing a soft and easy rendition of *Speak Low* by Tony Bennett and Norah Jones. She was feeling good.

In a fraction of a second, four of the second floor windows and two doors leading into the judo room crashed in. Ten fighters in stealth outfits burst in and hurled half a dozen flash-bang grenades into the room catching the guard detail, Drake, and Cerisse, completely by surprise. Before any of the agents could get off a shot, they were killed by head shots from silenced machine pistols. Calandra threw her body over Cerisse to cover her, but two of the intruders threw her off and cut her throat. Drake leaped to his feet choking from the acrid smoke in the room trying to regain his balance, hearing, and vision. A huge member of the invading team hit him in the back of the head with a flexible sap, and Drake was knocked unconscious.

Cerisse did a kip and came to her feet. Her reactions were automatic, conditioned by hours on the mat. She caught one of her intended captors with a hip throw and landed him breathless on the floor. A second man threw his right arm around her small neck from behind and flew over her shoulders, landing in a very painful heap beside the first attacker. It was all for naught because five men smothered her and pushed her to the ground. She attempted to scream; but a chloroform soaked cloth covered her face; and she slipped into darkness.

Ivan Droskovsky ordered the men to duct tape her mouth and eyes and to place a black hood over her head. She was hand-cuffed; her feet were bound with leather restraints; and her wrists and ankles were held on a short chain leash attached to a waist chain. The waist chain was too large by half because the attackers had overestimated her tiny waist size. They had to improvise by making a knot in the chain and wrapping duct tape around the knot to keep it snug.

Droskovsky's men placed Cerisse in a black body bag which was partially unzipped to allow room for air to get in. None of the attackers was hurt, but two of them were chagrined at having been thrown by a girl who probably weighed less than 75 pounds.

Nothing was heard outside of Burr Gymnasium, and no one else was in the building. Two guards did a quick reconnoiter of the perimeter of the gymnasium and pronounced the escape route to be clear.

"Want to finish this one?" one the large men who had been thrown by Cerisse—referring to Drake—asked Droskovsky in their native Russian.

"No, the boss wants a witness; so, the Americans know who got their little girl even though they can't prove it. Besides, he won't wake up for hours if not days. I don't think anyone will discover this mess for the rest of the weekend."

Thirteen more Secret Service agents and four of Droskovsky's men died over the next 24 hours, but every kidnapping was otherwise successfully accomplished. A total of five highly valued daughters of American officials were unceremoniously dumped onto the floor of a corporate jet at midnight on the twelfth. They were extremely uncomfortable but otherwise unhurt. Cerisse Daniels—daughter of the DCIA—was taken from her workout room at her university; Abigail and Susan Margoles—daughters of Frank and Mary Ann Margoles, the Secretary of HHS and his wife—were abducted from their rooms at Georgetown Preparatory School, a very exclusive, very expensive and presumably secure boarding school—the nation's oldest Jesuit school and the only Jesuit boarding school. Even an eight man security team was no match for the fully prepared team of Droskovsky's Mafiosi. In the case of the Margoles twins, there was collateral damage. Two Mafiosi and all eight Secret Service agents were killed in the brief fierce firefight and four girls in adjoining room were also killed. There was no hope of pulling off that abduction without attracting attention. The Mafiosi had planned the abduction for weeks and had a nearly perfect escape route planned. So far as law enforcement was concerned, the kidnappers disappeared into thin air.

Gretchen Farnsworth—daughter of Cyril Farnsworth the DUSCYBERCOM [Director U.S. Cyber Command], a widower—was snatched off International Street in Tyson's Corner as she and her date were walking to their car after dinner at the exclusive Wildfire Restaurant. Two Secret Service agents died trying to prevent the abduction. There were only two witnesses. They described a black van with no license plates from which half a dozen people dressed from head to toe in black—they could not say whether they were male or female or anything about their race—jumped out, shot the two government agents with guns that made very little sound, and hit the boyfriend in the head knocking him out. Ms. Farnsworth was thrown into back of the van which then sped away. The entire episode could not have lasted more than half a minute. The witnesses did not believe that any of the kidnappers were injured in the brief encounter.

Jane Coombs-Hartvig—the two-year-old granddaughter of Randolph and Katrina Coombs and daughter of Georgetown University law student Patrick Hartvig and Logan Coombs-Hartvig—was snatched from her crib in her own bedroom on P Street Northwest in Georgetown. Two

Secret Service agents were shot, one fatally, and the other critically, in the brief struggle to protect the baby girl. One mafia kidnapper was shot in the left shoulder but escaped with the rest of the abduction team without a problem.

Senate Majority Leader Coombs and his wife were on a ski vacation in Alta, Utah that day. The kidnapping was not reported until two days later when the Latina cleaning lady, Rosarita Sanchez, came to the house on Monday morning to start work and found the dead agent, the badly wounded one, and the empty crib.

It took an unfortunate twelve hours to connect the dots leading to the conclusion that this was a well-organized multiple kidnapping of the daughters of highly placed government officials and nearly 72 hours to confirm that Cerisse Daniels was one of them. Television and newspapers trumpeted the breaking news as soon as the first kidnapping was confirmed—the Margoles twins.

As soon as she heard the news, Sybil called the Secret Service security detail office and asked what they knew. No news had come in from Howard University during the night. The last report at 9:30 was that all was well. While Sybil was talking to the duty officer, other staffers tried to contact the on-site Secret Service V.I.P. protection unit without success. Cerisse's location was not part of the report. Cerisse's implanted GPS chip was not working. Sybil and Charles called Cerisse's and Drake's cells and got no response. They drove to the university and rousted the campus police who mounted a search that covered almost the entire campus. FBI, CIA, Secret Service, and WMPD [Washington Metropolitan Police Department] law-enforcement officers began a well-organized dragnet operation throughout the campus. They were unsuccessful and widened the search to a ten block radius the following morning. Only when students walked into the judo room for their Monday morning PHED 014 beginners judo course was the carnage of Cerisse's abduction discovered.

House No. 6, Maly Patriarshy Pereulok, South-west Side of Patriarshiye Ponds, Moscow, Home of Leonid Aleksandrovich Zaslavsky, the *vory v zakone* [syndicate boss and chief of the thieves-in-law] of the *Solntsevskaya Bratva, russkaya mafiya* [Russian mafia], January 13, 2020, 0600 hrs

Solntsevskaya Bratva, russkaya mafiya boss, Leonid Zaslavsky was awakened from a dreamless slumber by his secretary who announced that there was a call from Ivan Droskovsky.

"This had better be important, Ivan Vladimirovich," growled Zaslavsky. "Tell me you have been successful after all of the television coverage of your exploits."

"Yes, Sir. Completely successful. We'll be home in a couple of days if all goes well. It is complicated."

"Successful is a word that begs definition, Ivan Vladimirovich. I presume that means that you have the girls and that you are not much concerned over the collateral damage."

"That is all correct, Mr. Zavlavsky."

"Good work."

Zavlavsky was not particularly concerned about the death of his foot soldiers. He had more than 5,000 of them, and they could be replaced. The deaths of innocents in America was probably a plus. That would show that even the United States government could not interfere with the operations of the *Solntsevskaya Bratva* with impunity.

Oval Office, The White House, Washington D.C., January 15, 2020, 0830 hrs
Present: POTUS; VPOTUS; DCIA; DDCIA; DFBI; DUSSS [Director, United States Secret Service]; DUSCYBERCOM; SENATE MAJORITY LEADER; COPMPDDC [Chief of Police, Metropolitan Police Department, District of Columbia]; Washington D.C. Mayor
Re: Investigation into the kidnapping of daughters of federal officials

After the attendees were seated, President Willets nodded to DFBI Grant Wallace.

"Ladies and gentlemen, I am sorry that we all have to be involved in this mess. It strikes too close to home for everyone here. I couldn't possibly know how terrible those of you whose daughters have been taken must feel, but I assure you that I and the rest of the FBI are very much aware and are doing all we can to find your children, to bring them back safe, and to arrest and see to the conviction of the perpetrators.

"This has been designated as a progress report. I am sorry to tell you that it is hardly that. But here is the report in a nutshell: we have received confessions by over a 1000 individuals, most of whom belong in mental hospitals. We have received claims from Al Qaeda, the Michigan Militia, the New Black Panthers, the Socialist Army of the United States, and the most radical wing of the Tea Party—called the "Year-of-the-Snake Tea Party Brotherhood".

"They all have extortionate demands for the release of our daughters unharmed and will kill them publically if we don't comply. Al Qaeda wants all Gitmo prisoners released. The Michigan Militia wants all of the blacks and Jews in the federal government fired—they list such well-known Jews as Sybil Norcroft, Grant Wallace, and Cyril Farnsworth.

The Socialist Army demands a list of over 100 new entitlements for their people. The Year-of-the-Snake group wants "Obamacare" done away with, all government pensions to be discontinued, the NSA, the National Teachers Union, and the Department of HEW to be discontinued. To get our daughters back, twelfth grade must be removed from our schools; Christian religion classes must be part of the curriculum in all schools; and evolution studies are to be taught only by the Intelligent Design organization. They refer to themselves as 'a populist revolt'."

Vice-President Tanner L. Oldroyd asked, "Could we hear from our famous Jewish DCIA—whose daughter is one of the victims—about what if anything the intelligence services are doing outside the country?"

There was a soft, polite laughter from the others in the Oval Office, including Sybil.

"As with all of the other mental deviants who come out of the walls when something like this takes place, we are largely inclined to ignore them. I do think there are plausible reasons to suspect the Russians and Russian criminal organizations. The unified national intelligence services have committed every spare agent to scour the rest of the world with particular emphasis on Eastern Europe and other hotbeds of anti-American activity. We are inclined—but admittedly with almost no direct evidence—to think that Russian factions have at least some involvement; so, we have our agents quietly but thoroughly searching. Like the Director of the FBI, we really have nothing to offer at this juncture. Like our fellow federal agents, we will keep looking."

The president asked Diane Radcliff, Chief of Police of the Metropolitan Police Department of Washington D.C., for her progress report.

"It seems to me that we must have more than our share of the mentally ill and chronic confessors. Besides the many hundreds of individual mentally ill and deluded folks, we have had demands from groups as diverse as the biker outlaw gangs, Black Knights of the Road, The Sons of Satan's Daughters, and one that named themselves 'The Uglies' for some misguided reason. The leaders and most of the members of these gangs have long rap sheets; and we have them under surveillance and under investigation; but, frankly, I don't think any of them have had anything to do with the kidnappings. They are proud to be criminals; and, in recent days, they seemed to have wrapped themselves in the flag as critics of the present administration; but the focus of their activities remains on rape, murder, human trafficking, intimidation, and the like."

"And extortion?" asked D.C. Mayor Ceophus White.

"Of course," Chief Radcliff added, "but essentially always for profit or as revenge for similar actions on the part of their rivals. I don't remember ever hearing of a kidnapping of a government official by these gangs; it is bad for business."

Senate Majority Leader Randolph Coombs took his turn.

"I, too, have more than an official stake in this set of crimes. My little two-year-old grand-daughter, Jane, was among those taken. My question is for Dr. Norcroft. Why do you think Russian criminals are the most likely culprits?"

"Leonid Zavlavsky is wanted for more than 300 murders in the United States; so, he can no longer travel here. The U.S. has no extradition treaty with Russia; so, Zavlavsky can operate with impunity in Europe, Asia, and the former Soviet countries. He has to depend on subordinates to run operations in America, and we know that he—as well as the top authorities of the Russian Federation—was furious when their plot to undermine the United States' financial institutions was identified and frustrated. They took in millions, maybe billions, in ill-gotten gains; but that has never been enough for Zavlavsky. It is no stretch to believe that Russian president, Afonasii Glebovich Tikhondnko, gives behind-the-scenes support for the Russian mafia. Politically, it is a sticky wicket. Militarily, it is impossible. From a criminal justice point of view, it is naiveté in the extreme to think that anything like justice will come out of negotiations with the Russians. At this point, it is my opinion that Tikhondnko is still smarting from his loss of face from his part in the attack on U.S. stock markets and will not budge an iota to help us find our daughters, not even as a façade."

"So, what are you, Madam DCIA, going to do about it?"

"It is under advisement, Majority Leader."

"Do you have agents in Moscow looking into it or planning an action, Dr. Norcroft?"

"The CIA neither confirms nor denies such considerations, Majority Leader."

She looked him straight in the eyes. Many an eye rolled at hearing the favorite of all CIA mantras.

Chapter Ten

Office of the Director, FBI, J. Edgar Hoover FBI Building, 935 Pennsylvania Avenue NW, Washington, D.C., January 16, 2013, 0800 hrs

DCIA Sybil Norcroft's office assistant buzzed her that there was an incoming telephone call.

"Who?" Sybil asked.

"DFBI Wallace, Ma'am."

It still chaffed Sybil to be referred to as "Ma'am", but it was so ingrained into the Washington culture that she had stopped fighting it years ago.

"Hello, Director. To what do I owe this pleasure?"

"We are going to stage a raid on the Michigan Militia tomorrow morning. Would you like to tag along?"

"Do you have a good lead?"

"I would probably characterize it as 'a lead' and let it go at that. But it gives us something to do. You never know what an FBI raid might shake out of the trees."

"Sure, count me in."

Grant Wallace gave her the details.

Office of the MMCW [Michigan Militia Corps Wolverines], Grand River Road, Farmington, Michigan, January 17, 2020, 0400 hrs

100 crack troops of the Critical Incident Response Group gathered in the sub-zero cold surrounding the militia head-quarters building, a run-down warehouse alongside an equally seedy restaurant. Aside from the headquarters there were no other buildings anywhere within a mile. The logistics were perfect for the raid, other than for the bitter cold. No one dared to clap his or her hands or to stamp their feet to relieve the cold. The 100 breaths raised a fog that made any grouping look like a minor geothermal hot pot.

Sybil sat in the command van awaiting developments. She had a perfect high-definition television view which was yellow-green in color owing to the need for night vision optics. She and the other ranking officers—including Grant Wallace—could also follow squad leaders who had personal forehead cameras attached to their night-vision goggles.

Wallace called the community line, got a "ready" response and gave the order to proceed. Eerie green figures carrying weapons ran in an orderly pattern towards the headquarters building. They were hunched over, keeping a low profile. The planning, coordination, and precision was part of their training since 1993—all to be as sure as possible that they would avoid another Waco incident. The action leader raised his hand and tapped his mike three times.

What appeared to be pandemonium erupted. Actually, it was executed with admirable precision and control. The front and rear doors of the building were battered down in half a second. A second later the front shock agents judo-rolled into the building and rolled flash/bang grenades across the floor. Following them, agents poured into the building through the doors alternating left and right directions and through smashed in windows. All of the lights in the first floor came on, then the second floor, then the third floor. Two dozen dazed, light-blinded, and temporarily deaf men and women, began to be herded out into the freezing cold. None of them had coats or shoes on. The sudden exposure to the shocking cold further challenged their nervous systems. As a result of those measures, the FBI team started with and retained complete control.

The warrantless, no-knock entry and containment of the building's occupants went off in a fashion worthy of a text-book entry. The only problem was that there were no kidnap victims in the place, no evidence that there had ever been such victims there; and none of the MMC Wolverines appeared to have the slightest idea what the FBI interrogators were talking about. Sybil and Director Wallace observed the questioning and agreed that they were telling the truth. The raid was a bust which only served to increase the profound distrust and loathing of the rural Minnesotans for the federal government.

Over the next two days, half a dozen additional raids were carried out in rural areas of Florida, Tennessee, south Texas, red-stone country of Utah, northern Idaho near the Canadian border, northern California and Washington State. All duds.

Sybil and Director Wallace made command decisions not to continue the program of raids. The cost and risk vis-à-vis the benefit was too high. The FBI, state police, and city cops went back to what they did best—wear out shoe leather checking door-to-door, following leads, and recruiting and learning from confidential informants. Sybil was not much of a hunch person, but she gradually began to put all of her eggs into one basket—a Russian basket. It was driven by deadly exasperation. She and Charles had to fight back the urge to scream when they huddled together at bedtimes. Cerisse's boyfriend—who would have been her fiancé in another week—spent most of his evenings with them following the news. The news came from people who did not know what they were talking about. During the day, Sybil had to be the picture of professional composure, and it was maddening. Her many efforts to make contact with Cerisse's imbedded GPS tracker were not exactly futile; they were confusing. Almost every time she tried to get a signal, the apparent position of her daughter seemed to have changed in an entirely random fashion.

It was not until January twenty-second when the first break in the do-nothing frustration came.

Office of the SAC, Washington Field office, 601 4th Street NW, Washington, D.C., January 22, 2020, 0900 hrs

A homeless man walked up to the front door of the blocky yellow-beige eight story Washington FBI field office and presented himself to the desk agent at exactly nine o'clock when office hours started.

"How can I help you?" the bored agent asked, well aware of the bodily perfume emanating from beneath the man's unwashed clothing.

In his mind's eye, he could visualize the fleas and lice crawling around in the man's unruly scalp hair.

"I have a message for the FBI agent," the man said, his voice mildly slurred.

"I am the FBI agent," the duty officer told him.

"All right, then. I got to give you this."

He pulled a slightly crinkled envelope from his coat pocket. His hands were filthy, and they trembled as he held the envelope out to the agent across the desk. A crumpled hundred dollar bill fell out on the floor as he did so. The agent glanced at the bill, then took the envelope.

"What's in it?"

"Dunno. The man what give it ta me said I was not to look inside, just do what he says and give it to the FBI man. He told me he would know if I looked at it, and he would come and take back the money and give me a whuppin'. So I never took even a peek."

"Can you tell me what the man looked like?"

"Nope. He had one of them hoodie sweatshirts on and a big heavy beard. So big, maybe it was fake. I dunno. He talked kinda funny."

After a few more questions, the agent let him go, convinced that there was no more information available from the man. He had building security take the envelope for evaluation before anyone touched it or opened it. The article cycled through the system for eight hours before it finally got to the addressee, "SAC, Washington Field Office".

It was five minutes short of quitting time when the envelope landed on the SAC's desk. He wanted to put in the "in" box for tomorrow—or even the "out" box—so, he would not have to deal with another piece of junk mail from some homeless junkie. But, he loved a clean desk and as often as possible obeyed the late, great, J. Edgar Hoover's dictum to clear off your desk at the end of every day. He sighed and opened the envelope.

The message was simple: To DCIA, Majority Leader of the Senate, DUSCYBERCOM, SecHHS.

The SAC might have ignored it as another crank message, but the sender had to know about the exact government officials whose children had been abducted. The impression that this was more than a crank letter was verified when he pulled out five 3 X 5 glossy photographs of children. Each child was seated on a chair holding a sign with his or her name and the date of his or her abduction. Every child looked terrified. Little Jane Coombs-Hartvig sat on Cerisse Daniels's lap. Cerisse was barely larger than the two-year-old, but the little girl clung to Cerisse as if her life depended on it. There was no writing and no indication of where the letter came from or where the pictures were taken.

"*This is the real thing*," he said to himself, and then he roused himself to action, the torpor of the day having evaporated.

Within minutes he had calls put through to each of the parents or grandparents of the children and to the heads of the law enforcement agencies charged with getting them back. Sybil and Charles Daniels were just finishing breakfast when they got the news.

"She's alive!!!" they said almost in the same breath.

A similar scene played out in all of the other homes and offices. But, the same sobering questions followed: Where is my child? What do the kidnappers want? How can I get him or her back and when?

Sybil said to Charles, "I am more than ever convinced that this comes from the Russians, but through so many cut-outs that the envelope will not be of any real use to us. I am going to send Mac Young and his deep-cover covert action team to every Mafioso house and hangout in Moscow. Ed Simonsen can mind the shop. I am going to Moscow as well. I am going to use my training and will be so disguised and have such a good cover that no one—not even you—would recognize me. I am going to find our daughter if I die trying."

Charles said, "Sybil, the president will never approve that. If you were to fall into the hands of the KGB or whatever they call themselves now, it would be a diplomatic and intelligence disaster. Think about what you know and the lengths to which those monsters would go to get that information out of you."

"I have considered all of that, but I have to go. All I have been trained for would be wasted if I did not use that training for this, the most important mission of my career, past or future. I have put lots of thought into what would happen if I got caught. I have my second lower molar cyanide capsule which I can get reinserted tomorrow."

"Well, Sybil, that certainly makes me feel a lot better," Charles said, his face in a tight-lipped expression, "have you considered me in your social equation?"

"Oh, Charles, please don't make this any more difficult than it already is. I want you on my side. The CIA and the president will be after my hide when they learn that I'm gone. I will need your help and support."

Charles could never deny Sybil anything she really and objectively wanted. He had no better option for how to get their daughter back either. He nodded his head in submission.

"How about if I go with you to give you a more convincing cover?"

"You know that's impractical. First of all, we can't risk both of us dying in the attempt to get her back. Think of what our little traumatized girl would think or do if both of us were to be dead when, by some miracle, she was brought back to Georgetown. Second of all, let's be frank. I have a certain skill set that you don't. I have killed people. I know how to do that."

It was the first time he had heard that. He tried not to be, but he was shocked. That statement of hers seemed to be the ultimate trump card, and he folded.

Sybil made her preparations over the next four days. On the third day, another letter came which was the clincher. It arrived at the Senate Majority Leader's office. It was a simple text: "You get your daughters back when you call off your dogs at the stock market. Give us a free hand, or you will never see them again. What's money in comparison to a man's daughter?"

That was all Sybil needed. The Russian mafia had her daughter. This was no bluff and no hoax. As soon as she received a copy, she called Mac Young, her faithful partner in most of her most dangerous missions in the past.

"Mac, you have already agreed to go with me and to bring along a dozen operatives. I want to add a couple of more experts in hostage rescue. Does the CIA have some real cut-throats who handle that sort of thing? I mean, the FBI is limited to the U.S., right?"

"Not exactly, but the FBI always has to get legal permission from the host country and won't go in without it. They are pretty obvious as they enter the involved country—they stand out like military sore thumbs. And yes, we have a few guys we don't talk about. They get things done; they don't get public credit; and they don't answer questions. If you go with them and me, you can't make objections. They will do what they have to do, and that's all there is to it. You up for that, Sybil?"

"For my daughter, I am. If I go to Russia without permission, I will likely be out of a job at the very least or go to prison for a very long time if the winds really shift against me. I will be in all the way, and I have to be the final arbiter of what the plan is. We can't expose our country to an international hostile incident. Russo-American relations are too tenuous already. Every one of us has to be prepared to lay down our lives to avoid being captured or identified as Americans."

"That's a given. Let me make a couple of calls. I will see you tomorrow at Andrews AFB at nine sharp. Come prepared with ninja stuff, disguises, nasty toys, and leave your heart at home. This is where you know you have to get off the porch to run with the big dogs."

Chapter Eleven

The most important weapon Sybil brought with her was money. She did not carry the money herself. It was just numbers. However, Sybil could activate those numbers anytime, and a person she designated could pick up almost any amount of cash imaginable. She came prepared to seduce confidential informants and Mafiosi and to subvert the much-vaunted, and highly over-rated, code of honor and silence of the *russkaya mafiya*.

Two days of nervous pacing on Sybil's part and a small army of trusted operatives—both American and Russian—produced a Mafioso willing to put aside his scruples for enough filthy lucre to take him away to a beach in Mexico where he could live in luxury for the rest of his life. Mac and the absolutely daunting leader of the special-ops hostage rescue group convinced the man that he did not have to fear reprisal from the *Solntsevskaya Bratva* anywhere near as much as he needed to fear Mac and his friend, and even more, the dragon lady, who never spoke. Sybil sat in an old imperial Russian chair like an all-wise Sphinx and held the Mafioso with an unblinking gaze. He acknowledged both the carrot and the stick and swore that he could lead them to the kidnapped girls without them risking capture by Leonid Aleksandrovich Zaslavsky and his minions.

Now that the team was in Moscow, Sybil was able to pick up the signal from Cerisse's GPS implant. The signal was stable and in a fixed place—central Moscow. Without the Mafioso, the team would be able to track the girl to 100 yard diameter circle, but the GPS device did not live up to its promise of precision of location within 10 feet. They had to be able to be more precise than that. The team's and the girls' lives depended on it.

The CIA ring leaders held a quick and intense conference and decided to trust the Mafioso enough to have him lead them to the girls and their captors. As soon as the man left the safe house, Mac, Steffan—not his real name—and Sybil quickly dismantled the safe house and moved on to a different location which their Mafioso "partner" did not know about. They arranged to meet in the forested area of Sokolniki Park at 0200 the next morning.

The cold was beyond numbing; it was frightening—25°F below zero. The plus side of that problem was that almost no one was out on the streets, and not a soul was in the park other than the CIA team and their "partner". Moscow is one of the greenest cities in the world; and, at that hour, on that day, it was one of the whitest. There are 96 parks, 18 gardens—of which four are botanical—in Moscow. 170 square miles of forest have been preserved in the city, most of which is in the central part of Moscow. It was easy to remain anonymous to the point of near invisibility among the birch, maple, and elm tree labyrinths contained in the two-and-a-half square mile area of the park.

The team was in place at 1:30 to be able to guard against betrayal by their Mafioso "partner". The members of the team who were to participate in the actual attack on the *Solntsevskaya Bratva* stronghold numbered twelve, and the rest of the team—ten men—was held in reserve and to provide back-up and communications. From their vantage point, Mac, Steffan, and Sybil could see out of their dense cover of trees to the large fountain situated just beyond the frozen ponds.

The Mafioso arrived exactly on time, and was alone—both pluses. The CIA team waited patiently for five minutes; and when no one else appeared, Steffan left the cover of the trees and walked in a circuitous path towards the man who was about to betray his *Solntsevskaya Bratva* masters. At this point, his life and that of the CIA agents were inextricably inter-twined, and trust became an empirical imperative. Steffan was dressed all in white and was almost invisible. The night was clear, and there was nothing but starlight to offset the mine-shaft blackness of the very early morning.

Steffan gave the pre-arranged signal—two long and three short flashlight exposures followed by a pause, then repeated. The Mafioso returned the signal.

"Everything still a go?" Steffan asked in fluent Russian.

"Yeah," the Mafioso said. "You have the money and the transportation out?"

"I do," Steffan assured the man. "I'm freezing. Let's get this show on the road."

"What means, 'show on the road'?"

"Just an expression. It means, we need to begin moving."

"I will ride with you and show the way."

The 'way' was surprisingly close.

The three vehicle convoy drove lights out and very close together to an affluent and very popular residential area called *Patriarshiye* Ponds [Patriarch's Ponds] although there was only one pond—a small, beautiful oval which was now solid ice.

"We are here; this is *Patriki*," their Mafioso told the team.

They were in a fairly densely populated residential area in downtown Presnensky District of Moscow with easy access to many of Moscow's most famous sites—the Kremlin, Tverskaya street with all its stores and restaurants, the Bolshoi Theater, and the Moscow Conservatory. Beautiful apartment buildings and a few large mansions were situated around the pond. The team cautiously approached their destination— house No. 6, Maly Patriarshy Pereulok, on the south-west side of *Patriarshiye* Ponds, home of Leonid Aleksandrovich Zaslavsky, the *vory v zakone* [syndicate boss and chief of the thieves-in-law] of the *Solntsevskaya Bratva, russkaya mafiya*. It was now three in the morning, a frigid January 26, 2020.

There was no activity in or near the house, verified by more than half a dozen passes by the team before they were satisfied. Mac, Steffan, and Sybil asked the Mafioso two more times if he was certain that the American girls were inside that house; and he swore on his mother's life that they were. Before the assault team made the final commitment to attack the mansion, they quietly circled through the adjacent streets—Spiridonovka, Bolshava, and Malaya Bronnaya Streets and Trekhprudny, Kozikhinsky, and Granatny Lanes. Cars lined the streets, but the team never saw one of them move. They moved slowly along the streets looking carefully into each vehicle and saw no one inside.

As the Mafioso predicted, there was no police presence. *Patriarshiye* Ponds was one of the safest places in all of Moscow—no criminal with any brain at all would even think of committing a burglary or a crime of violence in that *russkaya mafiya* stronghold—and the police had an understanding with the *mafiya*. Moscow is home to more billionaires than any other city in the world, and a fair share of them were in Paradise Ponds. House No. 6, Maly Patriarshy Pereulok was home to one of them.

The house was an old and beautifully preserved late nineteenth century Gothic/Neo-Gothic mansion located facing the pond in an island of calm in the heart of Moscow, which has more than its share of street crime. All low-rise buildings which once surrounded the pond had given way after the 1950s to mansions filled with people who did not fraternize with one another and who made it a ruling dogma of their lives not to know that No. 6 was home to the chief-of-chiefs of the *mafiya*. They went to great lengths to keep their neighborhood looking respectable.

By 3:30, the team had decided on their escape route and had found a lot adjacent to No. 6 where they could park their two SUVs and their van in relative obscurity. Christian Hanks was the electronics advance man. He crept through the snow up to the house and used the wizardry of his electronic devices to map out the security system. It helped that he was in possession of the blue prints of the place drawn when No. 6 was refurbished in 2014. With the help of a little *c. взяточничество* [bribery money] everything they needed was obtained from the hall of records.

Christian decided on the most vulnerable entrance points.

"It is amazing, but they have next to nothing in the way of security on the second and third floors. We can climb the rear fire escape then move along the narrow balcony to the second floor portico. We should be able to cut out a segment of the glass doors and get in without making a sound."

"Too noisy," Steffan said, "we'll have to climb the walls."

"How about human and K-9 guards?" Sybil asked.

"Probably there—both of them—but I didn't get detected by either in my little reconnoitering adventure. We have some ground steak packed with doggy sedatives to feed them if—or more realistically, when—they greet us."

He was right. As soon as the group of CIA agents got close to the house, three silent and very menacing Doberman Pincers rounded the corner of the house from the hedge area in the back. As predicted, they were more interested in the mounds of ground meat than in the intruders; and they succumbed quickly to the long-acting sedatives.

Mac and Steffan unfolded and threw their four talon steel grappling hooks and lines up to the second floor balustrade and climbed swiftly up the braided nylon ropes. They opened their backpacks and each withdrew a thin but sturdy rope ladder. Sybil and the six additional men—who had been selected to make the actual entry into the house—quickly ascended the ladders and joined Mac and Steffan on the narrow stone balcony walkway with its marvelous niches and frescos. They were all wearing the best military night-vision goggles available in the world. The nine intruders made their way to the glass doors which opened onto a small second floor patio. The other four members of the team remained out in the cold to patrol the grounds to protect against sentries.

The first death occurred less than a minute after the entry team cut an opening through the glass doors and into the house. A sentry, shivering in the cold and clutching a steaming mug of tea, walked into a trap set by two of the CIA perimeter guards. The sentry never knew what hit him. No one standing more than five feet away would have heard a thing.

Inside the house, Sybil's team reconnoitered and spent a few minutes getting their bearings. They communicated by pre-arranged hand signals and separated—combat knives in hands—to eliminate any security guards and to find where the girls were kept. Sybil drew first blood. She rounded a corner and saw a sentry standing in front of one of the second floor bedrooms. He had ear buds in his ears and was swaying to music coming from an iPod. Sybil's svelte figure covered in black slipped along hugging the wall. The hallway was pitch-black except for a small night light mounted over the bedroom door. She moved with glacial celerity and in perfect silence until she was standing next to the sentry who was absorbed in his music. He was little more than a teenager. Sybil dispatched him with a sudden swipe of her razor sharp K-bar knife. She caught his body as he crumpled to the floor before he could make a noise. She entered the bedroom, presuming it was the room of someone important because of the guard.

From photographs of the family prepared before the mission unit left the U.S., Sybil recognized that she was looking at the adored daughter of the most violent man in Russia. Renata Leonidovna Zaslavsky was the only child of the *vory v zakone* [chief of chiefs] of the *Solntsevskaya Bratva* and was an accomplished cyber hacker and criminal in her own right. Renata was easily the most protected adolescent in all of Russia. Given that she was the daughter of the *vory v zakone*, she was an untouchable. No criminal in his right mind would risk a six week slow death by disturbing a hair on the beautiful blond girl's head. She was a genius; her specialty was the placement of network viruses which could be used to corrupt information transfer or to disrupt the function of an entire network, something she had done to the NYSE computer network a few weeks previously.

Improvising, Sybil took out her bottle of chloroform, dabbed some on a black handkerchief and quickly and forcefully applied the cloth to Renata's nose and mouth. There was a very brief and violent—but quiet—struggle before the pretty young woman was anesthetized. Sybil bound her hands and ankles with plastic cuffs and taped her mouth and eyes with duct tape. By the time she was back out in the hallway, the other agents had shot and killed three other sentries with silencer equipped pistols. The guards had been posted in front of third floor bedrooms. All nine CIA agents gathered in front of the largest and most elaborate door, presuming that it led into the *vory v zakone*, Leonid Aleksandrovich Zaslavsky and his wife Christiane's bedroom.

That presumption was correct. The corpulent chief-of-chiefs was snoring vigorously. His wife—in a separate bed—had ear plugs in her ears and a soft black face mask over her eyes. On each of their bedside tables sat a half-finished goblet of red wine and a bottle of the powerful sleep agent, Zolpidem. Sybil chloroformed and bound Christiane. The rest of the agents surrounded the bed of Leonid Aleksandrovich and pounced on him. He was trussed up like a Christmas goose before he could mount an effective or noisy defense. At Mac and Steffans' insistence, he remained conscious; so, he could communicate.

In Russian, Steffan spoke softly and with menace to the terrified mafia boss, "Don't make a sound, or I will blind you," where Steffan's first words.

He punctuated his communication with the point of a knife hovering less than a quarter of an inch above Zavlavsky's left eye.

"Good thinking," Steffan said.

He removed the duct tape from Zavlavsky's mouth.

"No noise," he said.

"You are dead men," Zavlavsky said, having regained something of his courage and panache.

"We are not, and you are in no position to make threats. We have no intention to kill you, Leonid Aleksandrovich. On the contrary, we want you to remain very much alive. However, if you put up resistance, I will blind you and make you deaf—a condition that will persist for as long as you live in a prison in a faraway land where you will be a despised supplier of information. Your choice."

Zavlavsky nodded his understanding but still glared malevolently.

"Where are the girls?" Steffan asked softly with all the menace of which he was capable.

There was only a moment's hesitation by the mafia torturer and murderer who knew that he was helpless.

"Basement," he hissed, "but they are locked up in secure cells and guarded by a dozen well trained and disciplined men."

Steffan, Mac, and Sybil had a hurried discussion in the corner of the bedroom, then Steffan returned to his stance over the helpless mafia chieftain.

"You are going to call down to the chief guard and tell him to ready the girls for transport to another safe house. To prevent alerting the neighbors, he is to reduce the number of guards to himself and one other trusted man. The other guards are to be sent to their quarters. Do you understand?

You are aware that I understand Russian perfectly, do you not, Leonid Aleksandrovich?"

"I understand, but I know you will kill me or blind me as soon as I give such an order. If I get on the line with them, I will order that the girls all be killed immediately."

"No, Leonid Aleksandrovich, you will not do that," Steffan said with finality.

He signaled two of the CIA agents standing aside in their black face masks and all black ninja suits. They hoisted Leonid's limp wife, Christiane to a standing position and ripped off her nightgown. Steffan signaled two of the other agents to step up to him. He whispered briefly, and the two men left the room. In a moment they re-entered the bedroom carrying Leonid's unconscious daughter.

"Strip her," Steffan ordered.

Sybil recoiled but remained silent. She kept Cerisse's name and face in her mind, knowing that she had to do anything necessary to save her daughter.

One man holding a wicked looking combat knife stepped beside each of the two females, mother and daughter and poised the point on the woman's exposed belly.

"Now, Leonid Aleksandrovich, you will make the call. Should you say the wrong thing, say it in the wrong way, or should your voice quaver, my associates will eviscerate your wife and untouched daughter and leave them to die over the next two or three days on the floor. Now, do you understand what you must do?"

Zavlavsky looked at Steffan with the purest of hatred.

"All right. Don't touch my daughter. Somehow, I will get to you; and you will die for six weeks if you do."

It was an idle and impotent threat; and both men knew it; but somehow venting his spleen made it easier for Zavlavsky to make the call.

When he had given Steffan's orders word-for-word, he added, "and call me when they are ready, and the two of you are alone with them."

"Good," Steffan said, "we will take care of our business, and if we are successful, we will return and take you and your wife and little daughter to a safe place unharmed. Pray for us, *brat* [brother]."

Sybil saw the light of defiance fade from Zavlavsky's eyes. Four of the CIA agents stayed in the bedroom with the three members of the Zavlavsky family while the other five— including Sybil—slipped out and made their way through the dark halls to the basement.

The area where the five American girls were being kept was a solid and unrelenting concrete dungeon. Two guards stood stiffly by the girls, one in front, and one behind them. The girls were blindfolded and had duct tape over their eyes. All of them were handcuffed with their hands behind their backs except for little Cerisse who was holding the toddler, Jane Coombs-Hartvig who was softly weeping in fear. Cerisse was cooing a quiet Congolese lullaby to the frightened girl.

In the next two seconds, three things happened: two flash-bang grenades went off filling the concrete hallway with smoke, blinding light, and a momentarily deafening noise; two men were shot dead with silenced 9 mm handguns; and five CIA agents swept in and gathered up the terrified and traumatized American girls. Cerisse was still clutching Jane Coombs-Hartvig with all the protectiveness her little body could afford. Sybil ran to the two little girls and swept them up in her strong arms and carried them out of the dungeon as fast as she could move, softly purring love and comfort to them as she went.

It took several minutes for the girls to regain enough sight, hearing, and cognition to be able to appreciate that they were in friendly hands. The girls who had only been weeping softly in fear before the flash-bangs went off, now gave full vent to their relief and cried with emotionally relieving gusto. Even several of the hardened CIA veteran dark-ops agents shed a tear or two. Sybil wept unashamedly as she clutched her girls to her body.

Mac and Steffan recovered their senses first and ordered the girls to be freed from their restraints and duct tape. It was heaven to be free and able to see and speak, and the American girls were effusive in expressing their deep gratitude for their saviors.

"The fat lady hasn't sung yet," Mac said. "We still have to get out of here. So, everybody, listen up and do exactly as I say."

The agents and the girls did not meet any resistance as they made their way swiftly back to the Zavlavsky's bedroom. Two agents slung the still unconscious Zavlavsky women over their shoulders, and the rest took positions to protect the American girls and to herd the former *vory v zakone* down the stairs and out of the house. As soon as they exited the front door, they were met by the four agents who had been outside in the cold guarding against interference. Those three men and one woman were instrumental in hurrying the CIA entourage along because they knew that they would be back where it was warm sooner if they did.

Sybil, Mac, and Vera Ystremski, one of the female agents—and a Russian speaker—got into the back of the van with the former American hostages, and the Zavlavskys; and the rest of the agents and the Judas Mafioso divided up in the other vehicles. The heaters were turned up to maximum, and the convoy moved out cautiously. Sybil did a quick examination of the girls and found them to be somewhat in emotional shock, but otherwise intact. She checked to be sure that the two Zavlavsky women were able to breathe and that the circulation in their hands and feet was intact. Leonid Zavlavsky called her several filthy names, thinking that she was only a woman, and not a Russian speaker; and he could get away with it. She slapped duct tape over his eyes and mouth and around his ankles as an unspoken indicator that she was not "only a woman," and he could not get away with anything.

She spoke politely to him in Russian to let him know that he was not the only educated person in the van, "Я с нетерпением жду говорить родной язык с Вами." ["I look forward to speaking the mother tongue with you."].

After that, she left him to his own thoughts all the way back to the United States CIA prison where he would spend the rest of his life singing about the labyrinthine world of the *russkaya mafiya* and its complex interrelationship with the officials of the Russian Federation. His wife and daughter would join in the chorus, but separate from their evil father.

Chapter Twelve

EPILOGUE

Oval Office, White House, Washington D. C., November 1, 2020, 1000 hrs
Present: POTUS; VPOTUS; SecHHS; DCIA; DFBI; DUSSS [Director, United States Secret Service]; DUSCYBERCOM; SENATE MAJORITY LEADER, COPMPDDC [Chief of Police, Metropolitan Police Department, District of Columbia]; Businessman Charles Daniels; University Student, Cerisse Daniels and Drake Farrer, her fiance; Jane Coombs-Hartvig, Grand-daughter of the SENATE MAJORITY LEADER; Gretchen Farnsworth, Daughter of the DUSCYBERCOM; Abigail and Susan Margoles, Daughters of the Secretary of HHS
Re: Commendations for recent intelligence operation

Every attendee had had to sign an oath of secrecy regarding what was to take place in the Oval Office that day except for two-and-a-half year old, Jane Coombs-Hartvig. Everyone recognized the crucial need to keep the secret they all shared only among themselves however tempting it might ever be to applaud for the men and women who had saved the daughters of several of the most influential people in the United States. There was an air of excited anticipation as President Willets began to speak.

"My friends," he said, "this is the last quarter of my presidency, and it is with profound happiness and gratitude that I am able to share with you, my fellow Americans, my joy at the results of the mission that brought our beloved daughters back to us and saved our country from suffering severe injury to boot. I regret that I cannot elaborate on the details of the operation, but I am sure that you understand. Perhaps in thirty years—when the secrecy limitations are lifted—you will be able to read about what happened. You know about the part that involved you personally, and you can carry that much in your hearts.

"It is my pleasure to give the highest award an intelligence agent can receive to a most deserving special agent of the Central Intelligence Agency of the United States. I have to tell you that when I first heard of her caper—conceived and executed entirely by her own volition and in violation of every law and policy of the agency—I was inclined—like Truman with MacArthur—to fire her outright and to cancel her pension. Now, my only regret is that I can't trumpet the success of that mission to the whole world. DCIA Sybil Norcroft, M.D., Ph.D., F.A.C.S. is about to receive her second Intelligence Star, the highest award for an intelligence agent—one that is entirely comparable to the Congressional Medal of Honor. She is only the second individual and the first woman ever to win that remarkable award. As she so modestly puts the truth, she receives it on behalf of the men and women who work in the shadows and do rough things in the night; so, we citizens can rest safely in our beds.

"Our financial crisis is well on its way to being relegated to history in large part owing to the services—which cannot be made public—of this one remarkable woman. Our National Health Service will hopefully one day soon become a reality because of what she did along with her government health official co-workers. I personally—along with all of the citizens of our great country—owe Sybil Norcroft a great debt of gratitude.

"Dr. Norcroft, please stand beside me, if you will."

Sybil blushed and walked up to the president. He put the blue ribbon holding the gold medal around her neck.

"Thank you," the President of the United States said to the former neurosurgeon turned government official—the senior officer among spies.

When the guests were escorted from the Oval Office and to a small reception luncheon, President Willets caught Sybil's attention and asked her to stay with him for a minute.

"Sybil, I am all but certain that Randall Broome will be the next president and Dick Harris his vice-president. I have two secrets to share with you since you are my most trusted mistress of the vault of secrets and chief of the puzzle palace."

She smiled at his characterization of herself and her agency.

"What I have to tell you must never be repeated. I know that you know that, but I thought I should say so. Harris is very ill, and no one but Governor Broome knows it. They just found out two weeks ago, and it is too late to get a new V-P at this juncture. The best estimate is that Harris will have to resign for health reasons—real health reasons—before the end of his first year as the vice-president. Governor Broome has mild congestive heart failure—that's another secret—and his prognosis is not that good. He is a real American patriot with the good of the nation foremost in his mind in everything he does. He and I have discussed the possibility of him appointing you to succeed Harris when the time comes."

"That is something of a shock. I guess I can't really say that I have never had a political job; but at least, it is correct that I have never had an elective position. I would be proud to serve if asked. Mr. President, I would do anything for you."

"Thank you for that, Sybil. You know that—if you become the vice-president—you will be the first woman ever to do so, just like you became the first woman DCIA. Who knows? You are very unlikely to become the First Lady, but maybe you will be the First Among Ladies—the President of the United States. I don't think your career is over, yet, my friend."

"Who knows?" Sybil said, "who knows?"

-The End-

Carl Douglass,
Famous American Writer
and
Media Personality